Cloth

By Caleb Drewelliot Sims

Table Of Contents

Forward

This book is dedicated to my mother and my stepfather. They encouraged my writing and the possibilities it could create for my life. I would be nothing without their help, love, and support. I love you guys. Thank you for believing in me.

Book Cover by Chloe Worthy

Closet

As their lips pressed together, his tongue encircled the inside of the other man's cheek. Tongues passing back and forth. Over and atop each other. Slowly sliding down with a carefully placed kiss on the corner of his boyfriend's mouth. Then to the cheek. Then to the…wait.

"Is that a hickey?"

"What?"

The mood was killed. Defiled by the act of a cheater caught. The night carried on with an argument and slammed cupboards. Then the doors. He would sleep alone tonight. The next day came and went without a blur. He felt everything. How many times must he start over the man thought? Finding love was hard out here. Especially since he was not even out of the closet to his family yet. What could he do? They all could tell he had some sugar in his tank. Just not exactly how much.

Time would be a terrible telltale sign for him. Growing up, his parents pressured him to be gay. So he was straight. At least kind of. He would fantasize about some of his cuter classmates. Though he would never admit it. The whole gay pride movement losing his respect. Especially with parents who pushed their nontraditional lifestyle on him and his siblings.

He was sad. Hell was a cold and lonely place. His only grace silk from a spider's ass. These dating apps held no luck for him. Eventually they would always leave. Now a moment of self-reflection would prove that he was the problem. Yet he was not there in its entirety, yet.

About a week later his problems had faded away with constant drinking and meandering with friends. Those around him only slightly aware of where his heart sat. They did not judge. They did not care. They just wanted to see their friend okay. The same thing his family said. Except these friends seemed to show it better.

Downing a beer and chasing it with a stogie the man in the closet talked with his friends. This time about his latest failed relationship. To them all though it was just another notch on his belt. Surely he would learn in time?

"You still trippin' over that hickey?"

"Which one?"

He said cracking open another beer. The day was long but these nights alone were longer. How could he love himself? Did he truly like men? Or did his parents want a gay child? All his life until now he had dated the opposite sex. Now as he was older, he started to give into his base urges.

He so desperately wanted to suck a cock. The idea of it, just the thought, got him as hard as a tire iron. He was just as straight too. He needed to call it a night. He said good night to his friends and went to sleep on the couch. Hopefully tomorrow was a better day. Not that the day was worse than any other. He still held onto hope.

Waking up Closet brushed sperm off his teeth and proceeded to get dressed without showering. He just wanted to move forward one step at a time. These flings meaning nothing to him but the world. Getting smaller as time passed on in the day. He ended it by hanging out with his friends as always.

"What was different with this one?"

"He wasn't funny just hot."

The revelation that Closet was actually trying to accept his sexuality was not lost on his neighbor. All he knew however was that Closet needed to explore this path on his own. Help and guidance would come of course. Closet just had a long path ahead of him. Especially when thinking of his family. Oh how they would cry tears of joy to know their son was gay. Closet sighed.

Closet did not know how many days had passed since his last fling. All he knew was that he was tired. So tired he should tattoo it on his body. Maybe as a tramp stamp? Just a thought. Lighting his room was a single lamp upon a table next to the bed. The bed being where he spent most of his time with these men.

Honestly, he was too embarrassed to take any of them out on a real date. He could not care about them enough. What if word got back to his family? He knew how they would react. Closet hated this facet of life. There was no good way for him to be himself. At least that is how he felt.

The pressure his parents applied for him to be gay was like choosing a purse. He could only imagine what the future would be like with gene editing. Was it nature? Was it nurture? He heard somewhere that it was booth. Only time would tell. As for right now, Closet just needed someone to hold him.

His promiscuity started as a result of getting laid off. Budget cuts in his department had left him without a job. He collected unemployment. It was enough to keep him afloat.

That and his friends helped out where they could. He learned to ask for help at a young age. A behavior he hated.

He wished to outgrow his need for help. To be self sustaining. However, that was not his reality. His reality was that he needed help. He could always ask for it. This meant to him that he had something to prove. He hated how he relied on others for happiness. He hated how he could not love himself the way others did.

Since he did not love himself as well, he did not know how to show love to others. All he could be was genuine. This took a toll on the young man's mind. One that required assistance. Going to bed he would pray the gay away. It did no good. Any drug he took convinced himself he was straight. Until he would look in the mirror sober and feel sorrow for the face of the boy looking back at him.

Waking up from a dreamless sleep, Closet went to the bathroom. Getting his day started was as simple as washing his face. He decided that today he was going to go to a bar with his friends. He needed some time away from his bed. Not that he needed to drink. In fact it was the opposite. He would be the designated driver. Making sure his friends got home safely.

Putting on his deodorant and a dress shirt Closet called his neighbors. On the phone he saw who all was going. Looks like it would just be 3 of them. Closet, His neighbor and his girlfriend. The bar choices were uninteresting. All just places to drink and meet people. Grabbing his car keys he walked across the street.

Greeting his neighbors at the door, they started small talk. They left without even smoking a blunt. Closet was dead sober as the night went on. He met plenty of dicks and pussies who wanted him. One did stand out however. Her name lost to him as she reminded him of his first love.

What a conundrum to be in. Closet being gay had set his sights on a lady. They all went home peacefully at the end of the night. It was just that now Closet had even more problems with his self. He knew he could not be attracted to her for more than a night. He knew how it would end.

Was this God helping him pray the gay away? Or was he still in denial? The sad truth of the matter was that sexuality is a spectrum. Closet could choose to be gay or straight. So was he either? These thoughts gnawed at his brain as Olney's lesions do. Laying awake at night thinking of the girl that made him laugh. He knew he needed to be with a guy. It was just so much easier to be with a woman. Another reason why he was in the closet.

He did not want to be gay. He did not want to be straight. He wanted to be himself. For that to happen he knew he needed to be with a man. That is what he fantasized about. The right girl could get his cock hard. Sucking dick made his cock harder.

If he could not get off he always had gay solo porn to shoot loads to. He was in denial; Closet knew who he was as much as others knew him. What a problem to have. Not enough dick to go around.

"What the fuck?"

He thought to himself. Is there any way to make things right? At one point he even thought about being trans. Maybe it would help him understand the world better. He just did not want to lose his dick or gain tits. Empathy. All he wanted to learn was empathy. For his problems and others.

At the end of the night he would always ask.

"God, why do I like men?"

Obviously he received no answer. The next few days came and went without purpose. Closet, still reeling from his identity crisis had stayed celibate for about a week. Anybody with a dick knew that feat. Instead, he spent his time filling out his resume. Eventually he had to get off unemployment. One good thing about being on unemployment was that there were no random drug tests. While fired he enjoyed some marijuana cigarettes. Hell, he was smoking one as we speak.

With enough exercise he would burn the THC out of his system for the intro drug test. With his next career opportunity Closet decided to branch out into a different field. Shying away from over gratifying himself, Closet typed on the computer. It was a list of traits he was proud of. Work ethic being the main trait. Here Closet was enjoying the now while preparing for his future. The only subtlety being that marijuana was not legal yet.

Finishing up his resume Closet saved it on his computer and began to look for jobs. Preferably along stem or assembly line fields. obviously, there were the minor jobs such as being on the line or call center support. Hoping for something better Closet pressed on.

High as hell, Closet found a job title that sounded almost perfect. Intro level webpage design. No experience necessary it said in parentheses. Perfect for him. He could be something he always wanted to be. Good with computers was a general skill everyone his age grew up with. Now while he knew little about web design, Closet knew how to bullshit.

No experience necessary usually meant work experience and he had neither. Fuck he had smoked. How much time would it take to clear his system. Usually a month. He could do it in a week. He sent in his resume. Trial by fire. Sometimes pressure was the best teacher.

The weird thing about Closet was that he liked women when he was high. None of his relationships lasted however. When he was sober he knew he liked men. He just hated to admit it. All his parents cared about was their image. Not his feelings. Hence why he was still in the closet. Who could help him? Anybody?

No matter how much acceptance he was shown. None of it mattered unless he accepted himself. As he laid himself down to go to sleep. His thoughts wandered. Meandering back and forth between his sexuality and the funny girl he met. How could life be so cruel. If everything is a choice then what is destiny? Only God knows.

His mind screamed in anguish that night. He felt as if he had no one. Which was not the case. However, depression and confusion had sunk his self into woe. Thinking about what he could change, Closet's mind drifted away from his sexuality to his affinity for doping his self-up. He loved drugs for the escape they provided him.

Perplexed at his admission of guilt, closet did not want to give up drugs any less. Alcohol, marijuana, cigarettes, pills. He had his favorites. Some could even say busting nuts was a drug of choice. It all depended on the addict.

All closet wanted was to feel loved for the way he was. Smoking and doing drugs hid that part of his self away from others. They made him seem confident and full of his self. All he really wanted was a hug and to be told everything was okay. The way people felt about themselves.

"This world is fucked."

Closet thought to his self as he laid quietly on his bed. Closet had everything and anything he could ever want. Yet it was not enough for him to be able to accept himself. Kids around him he went to school with dying. Growing up and starting families. Dying again. All bigger, realer, actual problems in the world. Gay marriage was already legalized and he still was confused on his sexuality.

Closet hated the fact he was who he was. A lover. What does a lover know when at war with themselves? To Closet it was pain, hurt, anguish even. Tears of joy would roll down his face. Happy to be able to healthily cry. The lover cried his self to sleep. Hoping and praying to be able to accept who he was. That night his dreams showed him peace and terror. Only being comforted by the fact he was getting rest.

He did not know he was dreaming but the sleep after a delicate sob had rid his heart of some of his pain. Why could he not love himself? Why did this affect all his relationships? The answer was obvious. It became a painful truth where ignorance was bliss.

Waking up was like a breath of fresh air for Closet. Not knowing if he would get anything right today, he started his routine as normal. Fixing his bed. Brushing his teeth. Taking his meds. Then washing his face. All a routine to make sure he was committed to being awake. Otherwise Closet would sleep all day every day.

Depression was real. Closet tried his best to be there for his friends. even Though dealing with his own mental health. Now whether or not he actually was was up for debate. Sometimes his love came across as harsh or not at all. Not being a breakfast person Closet had a banana and a glass of milk. Following he did 15 push ups and 30 crunches. All to stay in shape as he was getting older.

Still only in his early life, Closet planned for the future. A future where he was old and surrounded by loved ones. No matter who they may be. Friend, Foe, or family. Starting the day off already Closet had to get his mind straight. Yes, keep your enemies close but to love them? That was something he had only known Jesus to do. He was not Jesus. Hell, he was not even Christian. All he knew was that he was himself. For some people, friends or family… that was not enough. So, to him it felt as if it would never be.

How so many people come to terms with their sexuality so early was a boon to his. If anybody could do it then he could too. He just wondered how to keep it a secret. Hungry, Closet was hungry. Not just for a better life. He hated eating breakfast. The most important meal of the day had the worst food choices. The best foods for breakfast were cereal and oatmeal. Both of which were not satisfying compared to anything else.

How hungry was he? Hungry enough to wait for lunch. He would eat around then. Closet had practiced fasting unintentionally. It was called growing up below middle class. Having seen what poor actually was, Closet knew just because he did not have everything did not mean he was poor. Just some days he was hungry.

Finishing his banana Closet got up and went outside his apartment. Going for walks helped calm his anxious mind. There was a trail close by with a view overlooking a body of water. He nor I could tell you whether it was a lake or a river. Sitting down and watching the water. So calm yet so dangerous. Powerful was the word for describing this body.

No matter how much gear he could put on, he knew he would not ever go to the bottom. There were things, creatures, at the bottom of this water. Fish the size of minivans. Things he did not want to see or believe. The view was beautiful. The water instilled a sense of peace in him. Peace and respect. A respect born of fear.

How many people had lost their lives to this water? It was only a shallow jump into the deepest depths. So many people could be lying at the bottom. Closet wondered how many of them were dealing with what he was going through. A family so accepting of your sexuality they prayed for it to happen. Even before he was born.

A first world problem he thought. Sitting on a bench he watched as birds flew, nested, and graced across his field of view. Peaceful, so peaceful. He even watched the ducks as they raped each other in courtship. The animal kingdom was for a lack of better words debased. Actions performed by animals were not governed by the laws of man. They were solely by the laws of nature.

Closet wondered how many dead raped ducks sat at the bottom of the body of water. Noting all this with the breeze brought him more peace. Peace that he could do better. He was a human being dammit! An animal but a man no less. These thoughts lasted the walk to his apartment. There he sunk back into his mind.

He was still unemployed. The position he applied for had never responded. Damn. This probably was a blessing in disguise as he could not pass a drug test anyways. One thing at a time he thought. As long as the unemployment checks still hit he was sure he would be fine. The money he made off work was comparable to what he made on the job. He did not have to work at all for it. A trap is what it felt like. This could not last forever. For right now…it was enough.

Closet's friends had called and asked him to hang out today. This was a usual occurrence. Together they sat on the porch. Shot the shit. Asking about each others days had them pouring their hearts out over a fire. Meditating over a speech greater than answers given. Tears were poured as beers flowed freely. It was all love. Love in its purest, brotherly form. Love between 2 friends. As the rest slowly went inside, the 2 had alone time again. They began to speak. The alcohol opening them up. Closet went first.

"I love you brother."

“I love you too.”

“Life fucking sucks right now man. I can’t get anything right!”

“Dude same here. My girl keeps bitching at me.”

“At least you can love a woman.”

“You still caught up on that?”

“Dude I fucking hate myself.”

“All you gotta remember is how many people love you man.”

“What does it matter? I don’t love myself.”

Not knowing what to say to that, his friend gave Closet a hug. Everybody decided they were going to crash or head home soon. Closet got up and walked to his car. He should not be driving.

Closets car keys scraped against the keyhole of his sedan’s front door. He settled himself into his car and closed the door. Still feeling the effects of the alcohol he decided he needed to go home. Hell he could have called an uber. He was acting selfishly. He just wanted to be in his bed. Away from everything and everyone.

Twisting the key in the ignition his car turned over. Slowly pulling away from the curb, Closet was on the way home. He was Falling in and out of sleep while driving. Closet puffed on a cigarette to keep his eyes open. He did not smoke. He had no idea why he was driving right now. Just that he was upset. He was not even a bad drunk. He was just tired.

Pulling into his driveway closet had made it back to the apartment. Noticing no damage on the car except for a curbed tire he proceeded to make his way up the stairs. He was stumbling.

Who could he convince in his sorrow? Thankfully he was not pulled over by the law. That would have given his life tangible problems. Such as a felony charge or a bullet to the chest. All depending on the swift hand that proclaims justice. Looking at himself in the reflection of his mind's eye.

Closet decided he needed to get a therapist. Otherwise, he could have just gotten himself or worse, others, killed. He hated how his family knew he was gay. Gay and still attracted to women. Just not entirely. He knew nothing. He could think of a million things the therapist would say to him. Not one of them could be true.

He always thought about how his problems could just go away when he smoked. Yet now would not be the time. He very much so needed a job. One where he could afford his rent and get his life back on track. Maybe discussing his sexuality would help. All he knew for right now was that he needed to sleep.

Waking up was a little better the next day for Closet had a plan. His idea last night to get a therapist stuck with him. He scheduled an appointment with his primary care doctor. After some time that appointment transitioned into his first official meeting with a licensed therapist. His therapist.

The day came when it was time for Closet to attend his first session. He showered, brushed his teeth, and made his way to the appointed building. It was under the department of mental health. Not knowing what to expect or who to expect.

Closet parked his car and proceeded through the front doors. Towards the front desk. In there he met a woman who introduced herself. His appointment was not for another 15 minutes. Sitting in the waiting room his anxiety started to sky rocket. He knew nothing about therapists. Only that they sometimes worked. Soon enough his name was called by a petite young lady. He headed into a backroom.

Once inside he was gestured to sit down in a chair at the front of her desk. As soon as he was seated so was the lady who addressed herself as his therapist. Closet was

Shocked that someone so young could be a therapist. She must have been fresh out of school.

This was ridiculous… how could someone with barely any more life experience than him be able to help him with life's problems? All these thoughts accumulated in closets head until he realized why. He was attracted to his new therapist. To the looks she gave him to the flutter in her voice.

Both being shy, he knew this was going to be a problem. Yet he could not but help to chase the dragon. His insurance covered this therapist so dammit he was going to make use of the situation!

Sitting across from one another the tension was palpable. They both felt attracted to each other at first sight. They wanted their bodies pressed against each other. Missing the cue Closet slipped into thoughts of depravity. Oh, what he would do to this woman. She called his name snapping him out of it.

“Yes ma’am?”

“I asked ‘how was your day’?”

“It was fine.”

Returning the favor Closet noticed a gentle smile had swept across her face. Exposing her painted lips. Or rather a perfect set of white teeth behind her cherry mouth. all Closet could imagine was her pursed around his cock. She called his name again.

“Are you alright?”

“Yes. I promise I’m okay.”

“Alright. You just seem lost for you first meeting.”

“Yea I am a little nervous.”

“It is normal to be concerned at your first visit. We’ll work through it.”

“Thank you.”

“So why do you feel you need a therapist?”

The question caught Closet off guard. He had not thought she was going to be so direct. He thought about the question for a second before he prepared an answer. Closet decided to start off with how hard it was to love one's self. Especially him. A common enough problem he thought.

Eventually the conversation drifted into his sexuality and the pressures his family put on him. For him to be their gay son.

"This was a new one."

His therapist thought. Usually it was the opposite regarding parents and their kid's sexuality. She guessed she had not seen everything in her short span as a therapist. Talking about this point helped shape and open up a relationship. Between the both of them it bordered unprofessional. Only time would tell if anything sexual of nature would come of it.

Closet did not know what it was about this woman. However, he was questioning his sexuality even harder than before. If being gay or straight was a choice, then was he either? Sexuality turning into a spectrum before his very eyes was shocking to him. He wanted to get better. Now he was just confused.

Not knowing how to end the session he said his goodbyes and walked out of the office. Getting into his sedan, Closet made the trip home wanting nothing more than to bust a nut. Finally home, he made his way up to this room. Laid on his bed. Then pulled down his pants.

His cock semi erect he began to stroke it slowly. Taking time as he imagined his therapist in his mind. Picking up speed he began to moan her name. Finally with a groan, he shot a load across his stomach. Sighing he realized what he had done. Closet quickly washed up, taking a shower. Switching into a pair of basketball shorts he was ashamed. Did he really just jerk it to his new therapist? To him this was a new low. It would not be the last either.

The next few appointments would go like this as well. Closet would discuss his problems with his sexuality. His therapist would reaffirm and assure him he was normal.

He then would go home and jerk off to the thought and comfort of her. None of it seeming to be healthy in the long run. As for right now, Closet was in denial and holding on. He found a way out for himself to not be gay. This was through the love his therapist showed him. Accepting him for who he was. Showing him he was normal.

Closet had been sending out his resume for a few weeks now without hearing anything back. Over at his friend's house his main buddy offered him a desk job at a call center where he worked at. Closet had no choice but to accept as his unemployment would be running up soon. Not sure how he would handle being in customer service gave Closet anxiety.

Lucky enough for Closet his therapist had helped him see a psychiatrist. The psychiatrist prescribed Closet Vistaril for his anxiety. It would help half the time which was good enough for him. Maybe in the future he would be on something heavier.

As his day progressed on Closet carried a false sense of self-confidence. He figured since he was attracted to this therapist, he did not have to ever come out. He could find a relationship with a woman again. He did not know if he was truly gay. He did know no relationship with a woman would last.

This sense of denial heavy upon his shoulders. He could mask it with good news. Such as the call center position accepting and hiring him. That was a nice change of pace. Plus being sober minded, Closet was accomplishing a lot more in his day to day. His house was clean. He was eating meals. Most importantly he was going to see his therapist as often as he could.

The negative was that after almost every meeting he would fantasize and masturbate about her. Softly moaning her name in the darkness of his room. This temporary freedom of sexuality was a false sense. One that changed his view of the world. He thought he could understand every man and woman in front of him. In reality he was only looking at himself.

Closet's cycle of seeing his therapist and masturbating over her after became his new normal. His relationship with her had grown into one of a personal friendship. This transcended boundaries and made the therapy interpersonal and almost moot. During one session Closet was even sure enough that she would let him sleep with her. The relationship became one of interconnectedness instead of a professional one.

She received as much help from talking to Closet as he did her. He became her favorite patient. One she looked forward to seeing whenever his appointments popped up. One would fantasize about the other. They just could not admit it to each other. They would not admit it. Not until one of them cracked. The relationship would stay borderline personal.

One of these days she thought. Same as him. It was a personal struggle for her to maintain professionalism about him. As he became all she would think about. Other than her own family she felt he was hers. She owed a responsibility to him that she would not fulfill. Coaching him in his sexuality into ways to her.

Selfish. Yet they both loved every second of it. Every minute spent together was one where Closet could pretend. Pretend he did not want a man. Every hour apart was one where they thought about each other. Every day passing was one where the feelings and longing would fade. Until they saw each other again. Repeating the cycle.

Every week or so they would see each other and have a session. This went on for a few months. Eventually it turned into a year and so forth. By this point they were as close as feelings would allow. Closet knew nothing good could come of this. Yet he continued. Continued to press on. For what was life without the yearning of a false love.

Sadly, it was the truth for Closet and his therapist. They both wanted something they could not have. Until one day when Closet sat down in a rain of tears.

"Hey, are you okay? What happened?"

The therapist addressed Closet. Not being able to open up he continued to pour in front of her desk. She asked if he needed a hug. He nodded his head. She walked over to him and pulled his head into her breasts. There he let out a deep shaky sigh. He was terrified. Terrified of life. Of this very moment. Of right now. Her right hand stroking his hair as she told him it would be okay. It would all be okay she kept repeating.

Closet stood up at attention and looked her straight in the eyes. Eyes that said "You better not do it." Eyes that wanted him too so badly. Leaning forward he planted a kiss on her mouth. For a second she resisted, but she accepted it. Backing away she slapped Closet across the face. The line was crossed. There was no going back now.

Closet went in for another kiss. She asked him to leave. So he did. They had a lot to think about. This one action disrupting a year's worth of therapy. A year leading up to this moment. They both knew it was coming. They just did not want to admit it. She could lose her job over this. What was he thinking?

Infatuation was one hell of a drug. They were both head over heels for each other. The dam holding back their reservoir of feelings had breached. Out came a pouring of physical need and touch they were both dying for. After that kiss, they both knew it was not going to stop there. No matter what was good for them.

He wanted her and she him. Only self-reflection could change that. This was beyond therapy. It was two people finding solace in each other's grasp. Being around each other now would cause awkward blushes. Heart flutters. They had to keep it a secret. Eventually, during one of the therapy sessions, their love was consummated.

It started with a kiss. Passionately, as they had been waiting for the time to come. Closet's hands grasped at his therapists ass. Her's through his hair. This led to both shirts getting pulled off. Kissing down her neck, Closet unclasped her bra with both hands. He placed his hand on her inner thigh and began to stroke. Once the bra was off, he grabbed her by the waist and set her on the desk.

Pulling her closer to him as his lips encroached upon her. This all was a wet dream for the both of them. Her, as she soaked his fingers. Him, as precum stained his underwear. Sliding down while pulling her pants off, Closet could smell her through her panties. Embarrassed she tried to turn away, but he held her steady.

Slowly kissing down her navel into her inner thigh. He asked her if this was okay. She begged him to take off her underwear. Pulling them down off her legs he planted his face between her thighs. Breathing heavily on her. Using his fingers he pulled back some skin exposing her clitoris. He gave it a gentle kiss. Softly flicking his tongue across it while one hand curled 2 fingers inside her.

He gently stroked her g spot to the rhythm of his tongue in her lap. Finally she grabbed him by the shoulders and begged him to be inside of her. She wanted him as far deep as possible and he obliged. Moving between her legs Closet whispered in her ear how bad he wanted her. She was a good girl. She needed his dick.

He wanted to be inside her. Slowly stroking while their tongues interlaced. Closet turned her over. Both hands on her hips he played the game as he knew how. Her soft groans muffled by the couch pillow. They had to stay quiet. Finally Closet pulled out and came on her ass. With a deep sigh they both laid on the floor half naked.

They had no idea what to say about the sex. She could lose her job for Christ's sake. He had just lost his therapist and found a new lover. Another person to convince his self that he did not like men. Closet liked both men and women. Making this journey all the more tough for him. Turning to look at each other as they lay on the floor. They gently placed kisses upon each other's lips.

"What just happened?"

She started before Closet cut her off

"You know damn well it was leading up to this."

Not playing stupid Closet knew this was a long time in the making. It was a hunger that filled them. A thirst for each other. How did this happen? Getting up, the therapist started to get dressed and encouraged Closet to do the same. The emotional damage already done.

Tears brushed his eyes as he realized he was not getting better. In fact, he had backtracked to this moment. The moment he came to of both their accord. He hated liking men so badly he fucked up his therapy. The one thing for him to get better was fucked. This stress permeated the room and was pervasive in his head.

Tears gently flowed across Closet's face as he began to start his car. He did not want to be this person. He was that guy. I mean come on he just fucked his therapist. How was he supposed to get better now? Closet was that guy. It made him depressed. As soon as he got home he began to wail. Quietly enough so that no one could hear him. Closet crawled up into the fetal position on his bed. He fell asleep.

Closet's sleep was deep. His tears and sobs rocking his body to a soft melody. His dreams were placid. Not having to think about anything. He got the escape from his thoughts he deserved. Waking up the next day however, his problems were still there. He could not have a relationship with his therapist.

He liked men and his parents wanted him to be gay. There was no escaping this hell he had put himself in. He would need to brave the fire and walk through it. If only he knew how. Right now all Closet could focus on was his therapist. As he was sure she was thinking about him. That moment between them solidifying Closet's confusion as a man.

Once Closet woke up, he sat at the edge of his bed for a good minute or two. He had to make sure that he did not dream up the whole encounter. Walking to the bathroom he looked into the mirror. Seeing himself look into his eyes. He knew he did not dream the encounter. Fuck! He knew he was not in love with her. Yet, he could not turn down the spark between them.

All the good he gained from therapy was gone with one moment. five minutes of passion after months to a year of lust. Their relationship had changed. To Closet it was one worse for wear. To his therapist, she saw a future with him. One where she could convince him he was not gay. She was the one.

After a year of talking she had grown to care about Closet. Not to mention she was physically attracted to him. She knew she was not the first nor would she be the last.

Still… she desired him. The week passed with both of them distracted by each other. Closet on how to deescalate the situation and her with how to make sure nobody knew about their newfound relationship.

To Closet this was not a relationship he wanted. He knew nothing with a woman would last with him. A sheer will of force was what kept Closet going to his therapy sessions. Occasionally they would have sex. Every day they would discuss their problems and what were ways to fix them. Closet could not find the words to break out of the bind he had put himself in.

She was young, but was this the first time she had laid with a client? She was like one of those college professors who slept with their students. The moral implications terrifying and horrendous. Yet to anybody that would listen to Closet. It was a bragging moment. Again, everyone wanted to be Closet. Nobody wanted to understand him or see himself as he saw him. A closeted loser. Some of his friends told him he should get a new therapist. He agreed with them. Closet would tell his therapist this was the last meeting he would have.

Sitting in front of his therapist's desk, Closet's jaw would not stay shut.

"I'm pregnant."

Were the words she had said to him. Words he never in a thousand years wanted to hear. A million thoughts raced through Closet's mind. Was it his? When was her last period? Did she sleep with anybody else? Did she want to keep it?

"How long have you known?"

"For a few weeks now."

She replied.

"It can't be mine cant it?"

"I'm pretty sure it is."

"What the fuck no!"

Taken aback by his responses, she thought he would welcome a child. Clearly, he meant for his life to be his alone. Not shared with her. She was so certain since he made the first move.

"I'm getting a new therapist. And you are getting a DNA test for that fetus."

Closet told this to her. The appointment went back and forth. Her pleading with him to change his mind. That she needed him. She loved him and who she got to know. His stance was firm. That would end up being the last they met. It was a few days later, sound asleep Closet's phone rang and rang throughout the night. As always, he kept it on vibrate and did not wake up to it. He had his therapist's personal number and she his.

She dialed and dialed his number over and over to no avail. All the pills she had taken had not ended her life. She awoke, laying in miscarriage. Alone and desolate, she had no one to turn to except for Closet.

"Please just pick up please."

She begged and cried tears to God for one more chance. He never picked up the phone. Tying a sheet around the ceiling fan she made a makeshift noose. She climbed atop a chair. The whole time thinking how she lost her child. She was going to lose her job just like she lost Closet. Praying one more time her phone lit up. A chance! A saving grace! Looking at the caller id she saw it was not Closet. She jumped to the floor.

Closet woke with a heavy feeling in his chest. Checking his phone he saw he had 27 missed calls. All from the same number… his therapist.

"What the hell?"

He thought. Calling the number back he realized the mailbox was full. Something happened last night. Getting dressed Closet hurried to his car. One of the times that they had slept together had been at her house. Getting there he saw police tape around the entrance of her home. Inquiring with the officers got him no answers. He knew deep in his stomach that she was dead.

He could not provide for that baby and neither could she emotionally. Closet began to shut down. An officer reached out to grab him as he fell to his knees. The world was going grey. He could not see. Though he meant what he said to her, Closet could not help but to think he could have saved her.

Whether that was true or not he would never get the chance to know. His heartbeat started racing. After going grey, the world went black. He passed out. Not being able to accept the fact that she was gone. Somebody he wanted nothing to do with. Who manipulated him or he her. Someone who held an impact in his life was gone and he could not save her.

Closet awoke in the back of a still ambulance his reality a harsh one. He had lost someone he was not ready for. He also lost a future child. This was hell. One he was not used to even though he spent a lot of time there. To him at least. This would be a great time to acknowledge Closet's mind state had been getting worse. This was a straw on his back that allowed him to get the help he needed.

Ripping the iv out his arm Closet attempted to stand up. The EMT on board and a police officer held him down. They asked him to remain calm. He could not. Prepping shots of Ativan they stuck Closet once, then once again. The subdued high pouring like water over his body.

Nothing really mattered at that moment. besides whom was she to him? Just his therapist. This trauma had sent him spiraling to a depth he did not know existed. The ambulance started and drove Closet to the emergency wing of the town's hospital. There he was checked in for suicidal ideation into the mental health wing. Nobody knew that the placenta on the floor was to feed his child. All they knew was that this man just lost his therapist. Their secret forever lost within him.

He would never tell another soul. Why would he? To tarnish her reputation? As much as it hurt to admit she and the kid were gone. If he could cope with their loss privately he should be okay, right? This was a huge weight off his shoulders. Getting checked in was an easy process. Devoid of all emotion Closet was led around the hospital. An empty shell of a man.

They showed him to his room. Passing by he saw other faces in the adult psych ward looking at him. All they saw was another patient to talk to. Nobody looking at Closet could tell his mind and body were devoid. For a brief moment the life had left his eyes. Only to be found again. He had hope. Hope that he would get better. Still his main problem had not been solved. Only delayed.

His room was bleak. Empty except for a bed, some shelves and a bathroom. He was in the crisis ward. The tile floor cold against his feet. He was made to change into scrubs before he got to the room. All his belongings were taken and held at the front. They would stay there as long as he would.

From the outside in. it looked like the one person Closet had, had killed themselves. The truth was no less bleak. Closet was depressed and nothing mattered to him. What was the point of expressing himself if nobody was to believe him. His therapists, his parents. Both saw what they wanted out of him. They focused on those parts ignoring the others. The others being what made him whole. Flaws and all.

Laying in his new bed, Closet did not want to be at the facility. He needed to be there. It was only mid day and already he was restless. They would put him on some medication to change his mood. He was sure of it. Did he need the medicine? Apparently, he was on suicide watch. He did not want to die. His ex-lover did and now look at her.

Terrible for him. He was still in a state of shock. Shock that was destroying his ability to empathize with the situation. A human being was dead and he could have prevented it. If he had just picked up the phone. He heard it buzzing next to him. He did not want to answer it. To hear her voice. A selfish decision looking from inside. To everyone else, how could he have known? Yes he could realize it was her. For her to commit suicide…suicide? She must have felt truly alone.

Why would she put all her faith in him? To her, he was the one. Her love. To him, she was a beard. Someone for him to hide his sexuality in. even if nobody else would see it except him and her. He felt he was a terrible person. Nothing had seemed to change that since he met her.

All he ended up doing was hiding his true self from his parents a little longer. Fuck that. His parents knew who he was from the beginning. Closet was hiding from himself still. Focusing on religion, Closet could not find a single one off the top of his head that would approve of his lifestyle. His heart could not be in it anyways.

He needed to be himself. Something that proved to be more difficult the longer he put it off. After so many nurses came into the room to check on him, Closet finally saw a doctor. The doctor talked to Closet and diagnosed him with major depressive disorder. This was news to Closet as he thought he was great at covering up his emotions.

The only people he had to call were his friends. Even he did not remember their numbers by heart. He held onto the hope that his life could still be normal after this. Night came around as Closet laid in his room all day. If he wanted to get out, he had to attend the groups. Now it was time for medicine. He only had to take Prozac. A small enough pill that would help regulate his mood. Once a day at night, it made him sleepy.

Closet just missed the morning dose. Going to sleep he knew that the first real day at the hospital was occurring tomorrow. His first day in purgatory like confinement. Hopefully he could get help.

The morning light was not what woke Closet up at first. A tech came in the room and told him it was time for morning group.

Ah shit. His first group. Coming out his room Closet saw people seated in chairs around a carpet. The floor was linoleum. In one of the chairs was a lady dressed in scrubs. Except hers were washable and she carried a name tag on her chest. She was asking everyone questions about their sleep.

Closet chose a chair not too crowded by others and took a seat. Immediately the attention of the room focused on him. The tech greeted Closet and asked him to introduce himself. Closet said his name and that he was here to get better.

"Good."

She stated. They loved seeing a new inpatient going to group. It was a good sign that they were willing to accept treatment. Which he was. The only question being would he talk about his actual problems? Or would he brush it all off to get out faster? That was a thought that he and the staff had. the staff for every patient. Closet, for his first time in a facility like this.

The tech went one by one having every patient out in the day room participating. The names and faces were unimportant at the moment. Closet closed his eyes and paid attention to their answers. These were people that sounded worse than him. He could only imagine what they saw to bring them in here.

Once group was over a younger gentleman walked up to Closet and introduced himself. Greeting the man Closet introduced himself as well. The man had no family or anybody to talk to when he got out. Or while he was in there.

Closet learned over the course of the day that he had a kid with a fling. It was troubling the young man a lot as he was barely 20. How was he supposed to take care of a kid when he could not keep himself outside of these walls? The world was real to this man. A reality that Closet almost faced himself.

It was eerily similar how close their paths had interconnected. Closet was a noose away from being in the same situation. The man told Closet about his life while no one in particular listened. He was there just to make the day pass by. Like everyone else.

Once there they put Closet under a multitude of doctors for therapy. The next day it was time for Closet to have a one on one with a doctor on why he was there. He headed into the closed room unaware of what to expect. The greetings went pretty standard as far as they go. He was told the doctor's name and what to expect from an inpatient facility.

The male doctor made note of everything Closet said in his notepad. Noting this Closet decided that he would not tell him everything off that bat while here. In the future that could change. For now, Closet was scared and alone. To him, hell was a cold and lonely bed.

After their first meeting, Closet felt more comfortable with the doctor to trust him. He felt no sexual pressure from him or ulterior motives. The doctor did not receive Closet with a lustful eye. This comfort meant the world to the man. Showing Closet that he had nothing to worry about. Closet began opening up that day to the doctor.

"I slept with her."

"Your therapist? I thought you were gay?"

"I am but…ugh… it's a harder issue than that."

"So you feel responsible for her death?"

"Exactly! If I would've picked up the phone."

"But you didn't. That's no reason to hate yourself."

"That would've been my first-born child."

"You don't know that that child would have been yours. Do you?"

"No."

"Exactly."

"I don't want to be gay doctor."

"Have you tried praying about it?"

Those cold words of comfort shocked Closet back into existence. This whole time he was praying for the gay to go away. That instead of practicing and living his life. Easier said than done. Closet's whole identity was based around hiding the gay from his parents. Now he was diagnosed with a mental health disorder.

Who knows how many job opportunities he had just lost. A selfish thought considering his therapist had just killed herself. His eyes began to water. Out of frustration. Out of agony. He could not have anything nice. Anytime he gets his hands on a way of life it would leave him. Any new thoughts he could have were drowned out by his tears.

The doctor was right. There was nothing Closet could do to change who he was. No matter how many dreams Closet had or however many women Closet dated. He was gay. Or at least partly so. Just because he was good at eating pussy did not mean he would end up with a woman. Shit he could live the rest of his natural life alone, cold, single in hell.

He was not there yet. Crying in front of this new doctor was a test of faith. He hated being seen as weak in front of others. Even if crying in front of someone was the biggest show of strength he could offer. The doctor let him get it all out and asked if he wanted to be back in his room. Closet said yes and the meeting was adjourned.

This was only the third day of his treatment and already was it one hell of an experience. For Closet himself as well as the doctor. He felt like he found someone he could trust in this new doctor. Someone who when looking at him did not sexualize him.

On the fourth day this problem would come up. Closet addressed this with his doctor. How whenever he met someone, he would imagine a sexual encounter with them.

Not all the time just usually. This seemed odd to the Doctor but he let Closet go on. Eventually it was decided upon that there was some unnamed trauma from Closet's past. Before his therapist came into his life.

Before nothing could be pinpointed. Closet had no discernable abuse from his childhood. That is that he would admit. Closet was sexually assaulted as an adult. This was a long time coming as he was constantly lying about sexual assault as a child. Something he was ashamed about but had no understanding of. As shitty as it sounded, Closet's life was a series of cause and effect.

The cause being his belief that he deserved the worst. The effect being he put himself into situations where the worst could happen. Now did he deserve this? No not at all. Myself and the doctor both agreed on this point. Closet could not see that for himself however. Not at the time.

The fifth day in the hospital, Closet was set to be released. They had decided that he did not pose a significant threat to himself and others. Now whether or not that was true was a test of faith. His stomach full he got picked up by his neighbor. On the way to his apartment his friend asked him about his therapist.

Closet replied that he had another one lined up. That he was hopeful things would be different this time around. His friend remarked how crazy it was to have your therapist kill themselves. "Crazy". The rest of the ride home was marked by silence. Knowing he fucked up the friend did not say anything else.

Closet still felt as if he was a piece of shit. Not entirely responsible for her suicide. He knew if he had picked up the phone she might have lived a little longer. This was another problem to pray about along with his sexuality. Prayer only works when followed by action however. Somethings in life we cannot change. Having to do the best with the heart of the cards.

Still in Closet's mind. He was not gay because he could choose to be straight. The weight of his world deceptively laying on his shoulders. All he had to do was shrug it off. Hell, some of his friends were gay. He had already slept with men. He just hated that this was what his parents said he would be. Of all the things they raised him to be…

They were right about this one. Of all the things a parent could wish for their kid to be. An architect, a doctor, an author. Why gay? That is what troubled Closet the most. It was to him the equivalent of praying for a disability. As selfish as wishing your baby matched your purse. Something he hated.

He hated how his parents prayed for this. He hated them. Yet still he hated his self more. The days at the hospital helped. He became more grounded in his reality. Realizing he did not have to tell his parents he liked men. He needed to however. To confront his demon. His demon being himself.

There was nothing wrong with being gay. Closet did not care about whether other people were. Unless the goal was to sleep with them. Consent was the sexiest.

He just did not have it in his mind's eye that he was supposed to be how God made him. He had this image of who he was in his head that he strove so hard to maintain. He was told in the past that that was not what made a human, human. He did not want to accept the truth of the matter.

Now, lives were starting to be affected by his inability to cope effectively. What should not be a mental illness. An alternative way of life. Not even that much of an alternative lifestyle. Gay marriage had been legalized already where he was at in the world. Plenty of people lived the life safely and were loved. Loved by their communities and those around them. So easy to accept for other people. Just not himself.

They finally made it back home and his friend gave Closet a hug and drove off as Closet climbed the stairs.

"Thank God."

Closet thought as he sank into his bed in the same outfit he drove to his therapist's house in. insane how much could change in two weeks. He went from being in a pressured relationship. To being alone in his bed once again. He was getting better. Still, Hell was cold and lonely. Hell was cold and lonely.

Even if he threw a blanket on he still could not shrug off the emptiness of his apartment. Wondering if he should drink that moment. Closet figured he had enough to take care of at the moment without being drunk. A sober reminder to why Closet participated in therapy in the first place. He could have killed somebody driving one of those nights. Now it was just a year later the death carried over like dominos knocked over. At least for now he was sober.

Time had passed by since the hospitalization. With every day Closet grew more comfortable with his sexuality. More comfortable that is. Just not comfortable enough to claim he was gay. Merely bisexual. His parents had gotten wind and wanted to talk to him about it. They wanted to show their love and support. Closet hated that.

He knew the reaction they would have. They prayed for it. Not him. Sadly, his parents did not care if he was anything. They just wanted to see him happy. It would take a fool to not see what was written across Closet's heart. From the way he acted as a child to now. Something he himself did not want to see.

Even though now he said he was bisexual he only chose to date women. He still was not okay with his parents seeing the effeminate side of his masculinity. A feat that confused them. Yet it was all love towards him from them. A love he had problems with.

His problems with his parents stemmed from more than just Closet's sexuality. A lot of it had to do with how he was raised. By them and not. Not having a solid figure in life he could respect. Closet came from a broken household. He had siblings who wanted nothing to do with him. As well as parents who separated as the winds blew form their partners. Somehow they always ended back together.

His father would cheat on his mom she would hit him. Then as soon as it was over, they were back together. This did numbers on Closet's mental health growing up. Problems that were very evident in Closet's outcome. How he lived as a man. They told him they loved him. He wished they would eat a bag like a sea turtle. Not necessarily die. That might have been too harsh.

He loved his parents. He blamed how they treated him as to why he was gay. He wanted that part of himself gone. For now, to his parents, to the world, he was bisexual. Which would have to be good enough. Even if it was not good enough for him. He knew he was not perfect. He would never give up though.

Always striving to be better than he was yesterday. Something he found in himself after his therapist died. Somedays he wondered the sex of the fetus. Would he have a boy or a girl? It did not matter anymore as both were terminated and made into ashes. Per her families wishes.

Nothing he got a say in. Firstly no one knew of their relationship except them two and a few friends. Second, would he really care enough to have a say in what happened to her body? It was a sad affair all around. Made even sadder at the thought she gave her life for Closet's comfort. Not even thinking of herself as her body silently struggled against the rope. If anything had deserved to die from their encounter it should have been their egos thought Closet. While she might have been toxic as a therapist, she was still human and deserved to be alive.

He would be lying however if he did not say it was a relief to not have to raise a child with someone he did not want to be with forever. Selfish but true. Someone would have had to take care of the child. He was not nearly responsible enough. Hell, he was on unemployment for the longest. Right now he held down a job. It was neither here nor there. Just something to pay the bills that was not killing him. He had toned down on the drugs to pass the piss test and just did not resume taking them.

Bisexual. He was bisexual. Not a druggie. Yet drugs were an escape from his mind's thoughts. Drugs convinced him he was straight. Maybe that was because he was living a dream while high? For all he knew, he was trying and that should have been enough. Enough was never enough for him.

Closet was determined to show his parents he did not need to be with a man to be happy. Even if he himself knew that probably was not true. Sexuality is a spectrum they say. Same with neurodiversity. Like autism. Nothing was black and white anymore. Not to say that anything should be that way. Life is rough for all of us. Anybody saying they had an easy life is down playing their struggles.

Closet was battling with his parents over eager acceptance of his sexuality. Something so small it did not seem like it would ever be a problem. His parents probably thought they were ahead of the curve by having this mindset. Instead, it held back their sons ability to develop as a mature man. As Closet grew older he started to know what he wanted. That was to be happy with somebody. That somebody eventually turned out to be him wishing for a man. Even though he was still afraid to admit it.

Coming out as bisexual was a cheat to the system. He could date even marry a woman. He could ignore his nature. If he could choose to be straight was he really straight? The same could be said about being gay. Yet eating pussy did not make him as hard as having a cock in his mouth. What a problem to have.

Everything was taken care of bills wise. The pressure to be not himself rose to the top. Life was so good for Closet he had to make problems for himself. Problems that affected other people. Brought them down. Took them away from life. His unborn fetus haunted him. Haunted him more than his dead fling did. Something he was not proud of. It was a fact of his life at this point. Another problem he created for himself. A lack of empathy.

If he felt responsible for his therapist's death, he should feel bad about it right? Instead, he felt as if he dodged a bullet. One that could have changed his life forever. He was not ready to be a lover. Much less a father. Closet was not even a good person. Anybody that came into his life got fucked. Even if unintentionally, they got fucked. It was his nature to be a piece of shit. This was a depressing mindset that held him back in woe. A pity party if he ever knew one.

You could not convince him there was no hope in this mindset. Eventually we all die he thought. Everyone of us.

Why did God give him these battles? He believed in God if nothing else. A God that loved all their gay children. All of them except him. Well, for now he was bisexual. Something that only introspection could take away from him. A deep look into his self. One that he did not think he could do. At least not at the moment.

Another day formed in front of Closet's eyes. A day he could try to be better. Or, hopefully, himself. He did not want to be himself. He wanted to be normal. Whatever that was to him was straight. Which might be surprising to those who are hated for their identity. If at all. That was sarcasm. Another day went by with Closet getting accustomed to his parents knowing he liked men. It would not have been as bad if his parents did not keep encouraging him to date guys over women.

He smiled every time he saw blood in his piss. A sign that he made the wrong decision. Maybe it was an std from his promiscuity. He knew he needed to see a doctor. A new therapist as well. Life was fucking Closet. Fucking him well beyond a borderline personality. Fucking him beyond submission. The rough dick of God put a pep into his step. A step forward in the right direction. A direction where he could be fully comfortable with his sexuality. For now he was bisexual.

Maybe bisexual would be the last thing he could claim with his mind. His life held no intrinsic meaning to him. Everyone would just tell him he was confused. Hell, he had friends tell him he was not gay because he would sleep with women. Closet felt he had to prove to everyone he was more than what he presented himself to be. Whether he needed to in actuality was lost on him. Pussy was nothing special. Without realizing he was good looking, Closet would say anybody could get a pretty face with good pussy. Anybody.

Whenever Closet was in between a woman's legs he was bored. Noting that should not be normal. Not for a man his age. He should be dying to climb a tree with any woman. Instead, he fantasized about sucking dick. If only, if only.

"Closet, I love you if no one else does."

Says the narrator. Closet was heavily loved by his friends and family. Just not by himself. At the current rate Closet would be living a sad life. One of hunger. A hunger to not be who he was on the inside and out. His personality growing up was flagrant. Which is the whole reason his parents assumed he was gay. Which he was. At least to my knowledge. If only for a moment.

The day started like any other. Closet got up and brushed his teeth. This time a new lady laid in his bed. Promiscuous. He wore a condom. He ate her out even though she was just a fling for the night. All he did was treat women with respect. They all loved him for it. Thought he was a king. The one that would be worth holding down.

Closet broke many hearts. She was no different. Cooking breakfast for him and her, she woke up to a meal. Something dudes she slept with never did. She was fairly attractive. Chubby and cute. Someone with low self-esteem. That is why they both slept around. For the comfort of another body next to them. Underneath their belt and the sheets.

They were more similar than different. Aside from the fact they both craved dick. Her personality reminded him of a certain other woman. One who thought he was made for her. He did not want that reminder again. After breakfast he kicked her out. He would not call her even though she left her number with a kiss.

Closet's friends would hit him up to hang out later in the day. He decided that he would stay home. He was stuck in a need for self-reflection. Even if he told people around him about his struggle… it was minimized. They did not understand why his sexuality rested so heavy upon his head.

How many times must Closet sleep with women to realize nothing could ever last with them. A problem that others carried better than him.

She was not the first nor would she be the last. The same could be said about him. He would not be the only man she felt she deserved. Not realizing how disturbed Closet was. You could not convince him otherwise that he was the cause to the effect of death. He did not want someone else to die because he would not be with them. He needed to stay sober. Too many drinks had him covering his thoughts and emotions like foreskin. Laid to rest as many of these thoughts got told to us over and over. His mind as prolific as a serial killers when it came to bodies and self-hatred.

She had left and he was over her immediately. If he did not like being between a woman's legs then why did he continue? That was because being with a woman was simply easier for his mind. Not attracting them. Not attracting other gay men was the easiest. Closet was taking a path of heavy resistance. Every time he was with a woman for the first few seconds… he could convince himself he actually liked them. What is worse is he hated texting or calling them.

It was such a bore and waste of time. He knew he would not last with them. Even his first love. He was not sure if he actually loved her. He sure as hell never showed it. That was in high school. He remembers how excited he was to be in a relationship. Just to treat her like shit by the end of it. Simply she was boring. He held on however because he could not imagine a life without her. Oh was he young then. At least she did not kill herself. Actually, he did not know what she was up to. He would not check either. He thought about her from time to time. Maybe he actually loved her.

Nothing was ever the same after her. He did not know why. Maybe one day they could acknowledge each other peacefully. A pipe dream Closet did not want. A fly flew near Closet. He thought about how simple and quick its life was. Not without meaning. Every life held meaning. We were all here for a reason. Even through the denial and self-hate. Things not so easily overcome. Those with promiscuity problems held the same worth as those with porn addictions. Even though they would like to trade lives probably.

Closet had all the above as well as a substance avoidance problem. He used to use substances to avoid his life's problems. Now though, he was alone again. Sitting on his couch Closet thought about his work. He took a new job as soon as it was available. The reason it was not mentioned was because he kept quitting or getting fired. His turnover rate was high. he did not know how to hold down a job for more than a few months. There was always a new one available however.

Each time he was left unemployed he had a new half career ready to go. Prosperous was a good word to describe his life. No matter how much he lost, he always came back harder. All this stayed out of his mind. He was always so focused on his sexuality. A lot of his gains in life seemed normal to him. They did not go by unnoticed or unappreciated. They just came and went. If anything, he was consistent. His job right now being a call center support from home. He made enough to be comfortable. That being his bills were paid. As long as he had a place to stay he was golden.

Almost every week he had a different guy or girl in his bed. To the point planned parenthood clinics knew him by face and name. Sometimes he would be dirty. Sometimes not. He always left with some antibiotics. Never could be too safe or sure. Today was another check up day. As he drove to the clinic he thought about how lucky he was to have health insurance. Every meeting was free. Once you are poor enough you are richer than middle class Closet thought.

As he drove Closet listened to his new favorite band. On the way to the clinic practicing his best self. It was crazy how music could fix his broken emotions. It was all good. A lot of the times Closet would find synchronicities in his life and the music he listened to. Certain words sticking their necks out to find place in his thoughts. Stitching his psyche together. Everything happened for a reason. It all did.

Pulling into the parking lot Closet got out of his car and walked into the clinic. The tests went by normal. He let them know he was pissing a little blood. Turns out he had chlamydia. He did not know if the girl from last night gave it to him, or he her. Either way it was nothing new. Antibiotics were prescribed to him and he left after small conversation. Closet made it home safe. He cracked open a bottle of water and took his meds as prescribed. It would clear up soon.

Grateful for the break in his sex life Closet sat on his couch and took a breather. Slinging dick was such a profession for him he should be getting paid for it. Now would that not be a sad life. Getting paid to give his body away. Something that would break his soul even harder than having bodies on his mind. Both dead and alive.

You could not tell Closet he was not responsible. It was even harder to convince himself he did not care. He cared a lot. He just hid it. No one knew about their fling that would have dirtied his therapist's name. taking advantage of one of her patients. To Closet however, he made the first move. That one kiss changed 3 lives. Hard for him not to care. Sitting on his couch, Closet cried. Alcohol was an escape from his emotions. Being sober, he chose not to drink. He needed to feel his emotions.

Crying over it was him accepting responsibility. Responsibility for his fuck ups. The way life blessed him. He did not deserve it. His crying turned into silent wailing. His face contorted in peaceful despair. Closet needed to let it out. He buried his face into a pillow. Tears staining the cloth as they poured. They poured out of his face. His problems getting lesser with each stream. This was not out of woe. This was from loss. Losing a therapist. Losing a child. Not being able to talk about it.

Closet's meeting with his new therapist was tomorrow. Would he talk about his last one with them? He could not stand the power he had. Just to dirty someone's name after death by saying the truth. He decided he would not say anything. As the tears poured Closet thought of his parents. How he loved them. How they loved him. Wishing relationships were easier. With them and for his peace as well Closet did not need a person in his life right now. Nor did he want one. His body count would stay climbing as he was lost.

His relationships with his friends seeming artificial. They did not know Closet as he knew his self. They thought they did. What was a few years to his lifetime. Something they would realize if they knew him better. If anything Closet was consistent. A consistent worker as much as his fuck ups. They saw some of it. His feelings being pronounced whenever anybody was around him. He absorbed the energy around him and lit it out ten fold. He could not hide. Everyone knew how he felt.

Maybe not all the time. Yet, it was enough. Whether they were thinking of each other or not. Its proliferation of each bled out into other facets of his life. Sometimes he could not even comprehend the foolishness he fed into. His meeting with his new therapist was today.

"Fuck, a new one."

He thought. Just one to lose the game of life. From a simple recording to a fully housed section 8 development. The will to be better than you could astounded him. As he was one to abuse the government system. We barely know what it means. A disease of affluenza. The opposite begrudged on his mind. Only those that felt could see a glimmer inside Closet's headspace. His proliferation of drugs a problem among his company.

Closet's friends being worried about his drinking. Especially after the death of his therapist. Something they would never understand. Hopefully. Drugs were a minor escape for him. Somedays he remained sober. Others not so. When he drank he liked to smoke. When he smoked he liked to drink. Those were a facet of his mind. Closet being half straight and half queer. Amazing to others outside of his own head.

His liver hurt. Such a slight pain dragging his mental health out of a self-questioning woe. His love for others carried him forward. He cried all he had to cry and got ready for his therapist appointment. A new one he thought. The Vatican would have to tell him he was wrong. Which would always be a possibility. Noting life in every figure. Particularly tragedies. Particularly death in its travesties. Oh why could he not be someone else. A fragment of his mind forever scattered to the wind.

Anyone can do this. His self-determined grind through it. Fuck it's a passage of life. At current his friends have hid the alcohol from him. May God give him the strength. As it was. Readying himself in the car Closet was prepared for anything. Arriving, the doors opened. At the head of the desk sat a man. Middle aged. He gestured for Closet to sit. So he did. A laundry list of drug problems shown in his tired eyes. Living vicariously through his patients was a fantasy. He had seen real life.

Some people would say Closet did not respect his last therapist. The age gap might have something to do with it. If not… it was more so because he and her had a relationship. As Closet felt he was a piece of shit. That motherfucker cared about him. Closet discerning that from the first meeting. Love he felt emanated with respect. A human caring radiated off him. Something Closet was not used to. A change that he could feel off the first meeting.

Deep in his heart he fed into the computer as a main strength. Tearing apart the simplest scribbles on a page. A pen touched with marijuana is a terrible thing in a schizophrenic's hands. A pan ladened with alcohol marked a short life. His liver hurt. Closet was partly invested in his self. He greeted his new therapist.

"Hello sir. My name is Closet."

"Hello Closet. I am your therapist."

"Hello Doctor."

A mutual respect formed at the beginning. How high was he after burning on the sage? Pretty damn high. his liver hurt. He drank too much. Just begging God to let him live. One more day please to Mary he prayed. Please save him. A bottle of water has him back to it. Lovingly. The meeting was over.

The same pains of yesterday stuck in his head. The meeting with the doctor more than philosophical. They were real. It is hard to recall dates sometime. Closet had a lot happen to him in a short amount of time. A few years span is really the difference. Between the days, a few will be mixed up. Usually his activities stayed the same. This therapist being a change to his routine. Already, coping mechanisms held strong through conquered fears. He could pat himself on his back until he broke his arm. A sold progress was made. He felt proud of it. A smaller battle conquered. the first of many. A thought that warmed Closet's heart.

A period of woe conquered. It felt good to feel good. Not knowing how fleeting this feeling could be, Closet held on tight. Many days were spent feeling sorry for himself. Today being markedly different. Provided him with hope. Hope that he could feel and in turn, be better. All it took was some self-reflection. Especially on his promiscuity paired with drug use. Even if not as bad as it could be. His struggles were his own. To live through and make peace with. He wanted to drink less. To use less. Closet needed to stop investing his whole energy into one night stands. Easier said.

His diary would become his main strategy to dealing with the incessant need to sleep with people. He had more bodies than the cartel. Something any man would be proud of. To him, he hated it. Who wants a worn-out dick? There always was someone out there for him. He should know, he ran through them. Another notch on the belt for someone that would die to be with him. She rested on his mind. He would never forget her. Not that her memory was not carried well. Her family was oddly supportive to Closet as well. Not that they were told. She kept everything about them between them.

His ability to discern public nature did nothing for him if they were passed. He might have loved her. Definitely told himself so. Closet could convince himself he was any emotion. Too much dwelling took him away from the positivity he was feeling. It was a sense of peace. A golden light across his story. A checkpoint after the struggles he fought. He wondered how many bosses he fought. Hedonism still a prevalent one.

A deep sigh of relief exhaled though his nose. Relief or regret to the drink he had just made for himself. His body count was too high. to him it was. Dammit he was supposed to be happy.

"Too much goes on in here."

He thought about his head. In his head, responsibility laid its head on his shoulder. Anxiety on the other. Peace began to be found at the beginning of a bottle. Closet needed help. He hoped his new therapist was it. Feelings enamored him. Closet was used to stuffing everything down. Hiding his emotions and feelings. When he could not, everybody noticed. This was brought up with the therapist at their next meeting.

Closet had an anxiety disorder. One of many such people like him. A minor mood stabilizer was recommended to sway his anxious causing behaviors. He was struggling to accept the fact that he needed more medicine. At least for the moment to be normal. He had his good days. He had his bad. His coping mechanisms could only carry so much weight. While both shoulders were occupied. He could still find peace in his mind. It required pills. His mind carried no weight to the decision. It was just a surprise to himself.

What he would not give to feel normal. To not hide on top of other bodies. The insight damming. Closet, despite himself, held to a few good days. Not everything became a curse upon him. The mood stabilizers helped. He was able to sit down and focus his thoughts. That one day of pure adrenaline marked a moment. He was to remain on this medicine so that his days could be better.

The shill for modern America. What Closet grew to see as he had more meetings with his therapist was how beneficial medicines in tandem with coping skills worked. He could lose interest in his work while high. These thoughts were of interest to Closet. He tried to drop substances still. Since the first day driving drunk.

Closet was happy. As happy as he knew how to be. He could see what he needed to work on. He planned on putting a conscious effort towards his goals. The new doctors were working. Closet was happy. This being a peace nobody could take from him. It would be by his own volition this time. A scary thought. He would throw away his happiness for a person. His walls were showing wear. Crumbling at some places.

He used sex and drugs to fortify his walls. Now that he saw that, he could start changing. Change for who? Not whoever. Change for himself. All he wanted was to be normal. Who is normal however? He ideally was happy right now. An emotion that had alluded him. Wow what a feeling.

This brushed Closet's thoughts as a new door opened for him. He had a chance. He would try his best.

That was all anyone could ask for Closet. Even himself. Why was he happy? Was it a random day? A goal accomplished? Maybe both. It was hope. He had hope for a better tomorrow with a new doctor and medicine. His therapy working after a few visits. His parents were also on his mind. He was not close to them as he should be. A phone call could change that. He had only been happy for a few days. He was not ready for them yet. As he picked up the phone to call them. He set it back down. There was a day when he could call them. To let them know he was fully gay. That would be the day. He had not the strength for it at the moment.

What news would be better for them? Their whole identity as parents justified. They wanted a gay son so bad they raised him like a new purse. That bothered Closet. He was happy today. He was not ready to validate the people who gave him this problem. If they encouraged him to date a chick maybe he could end his trauma at bisexual. The sad truth of the matter showed no face to Closet. That both nature and nurture influenced a kid's disposition.

His parents not at complete fault. His problem with sexuality being very common. Especially among the community. Coming out was made to seem rough. More so back in the day when people lost their lives. Being gay had you targeted back then. Closet would have either been rich or a dead man with as many male bodies as he had. Closet had an affinity for dick. One that was hard to ignore. Like a cigarette, he wanted a dick in his mouth. How did they raise a child to want that? Nature and nurture.

He was still "confused" said those around him. They would talk about the female bodies he had. They were not nearly as many as the guys that slipped inside him. They were enough for his friends to believe Closet when he told his parents he was bisexual. Most people believed him. Most people did not care. The only person it mattered to was Closet. He could not see that far down the tunnel yet. He had hope and a light at the end of it.

Steadily smoking a cigarette, Closet felt he had found pieces of himself in the ash. He could see all his bad decisions burning on the tip of it. Letting it all ember away into smoke. He had maintained a steady life with his new therapist. His problems went fully from a high body count to how does he quit smoking cigarettes. Now alcohol still reared its ugly head. Same with the head highs of weed. He wanted to be done with it all. A tough battle for anyone. Closet felt these problems were nothing in comparison to his before. Not discounting himself. Being responsible for the death of another person ate at him.

His sexuality was burgeoning. He just needed to he comfortable enough to accept that he might not be fully gay. Or was that a cover up still? He had still avoided the talk with his parents. Now however, it felt like his parents could care less. They were just happy to have a son who smiled again. His alcoholism worried them. He thought he hid it well but it showed. Now this was not the reason Closet smiled. The drugs only brought him down. He was on a road of self-recovery and he felt it. Felt that he was turning a chapter in his life. One where he did not need drugs and alcohol as he once did. Now if anyone could quit smoking. Smoking cigarettes. Smoking dick. He did both equally.

He was not as promiscuous. That did not mean by any means Closet was practicing celibacy. Quite the opposite. He held a few friends he would sleep with. He just no longer hooked up with random men at bars. Women were a different story. He slept with a lot less women. Moving towards an ever-growing goal post. Something he loved about life. No matter how much he grew. There was always a goal to achieve.

The best part about the pursuit of perfection was nothing would ever be perfect until it was left alone. His life was to be lived as long as he stood. Plus then some. He was happy. Only he and God could take that from him. A loving God. The only God he could truly worship. All he knew in his life was love and fear. Love leading to madness to anger. Fear leading to a despot of others' emotions. He was terrible at times and he knew it.

Others looked him in the eyes and told him he was worth it. Worth being loved. Worthy to be happy. Allowed to be himself. Worthy of it even. Who would God put on this earth more worthy of being Closet than Closet? A pantry? Maybe a whole ass cubicle. One that worked as hard as he did. After everything was said and done Closet was still himself. He deserved to be loved by himself. He heard it everywhere. From his neighbors to strangers. People loved him. He was learning to fully love his self.

Not every day was a good day. That did not mean Closet deserved to come home to self-loathing. Quite the opposite. He deserved to come home to someone who loved him. Right now that was Closet. Who could imagine his hell? Most people he imagined. He imagined most people were good at heart. He had met evil in this world. Not the full terror that existed. Well that was a lie. His therapist, the first one, was abject emotion. Everything he ever could have felt went through that women. He almost had a kid. His smile started to fade away from his face. Life was real. Even if not, it was real enough to him. That is all that mattered anyways.

He needed guidance and he found it. It was in the doctors who helped him. His neighbors and friends. Those who showed him how to maneuver through his psyche. Most of them had felt what he felt if just at a different time. The good thing about being human was most of us felt emotion. So most of them could relate. Love was fickle. Trust was everything. He was learning to trust himself to not fuck up his life. New ground to be covered as his high was lost. Closet was not the man he wanted to be. Not yet. If God had his way he never would be. The constant growth a wonderful thing.

As a human he never could be perfect. As a man that was never good enough. So he would try. As he tried he would learn. Hopefully he would be allowed to keep living. Closet sighed at the end of his night. Enjoying music and his own company. He had gotten comfortable. No new problem had reared its head in who knows how long for him. Not that he was asking for one. He was trying to learn to enjoy the peace. His head being silent. Usually filled with wry remarks about the passage of those around him. Especially throughout the night when his day was over.

His jobs ever changing. That was a problem. He could never hold down a job for too long. Always something causing him to quit, get laid off, or fired. This last time he was fired. His attendance being the main problem. If he did not feel his time was being appreciated, he just stopped showing up on time. A job being a job. He did not care where they were or what they did. He just did not want to feel used. The emotionless slap of the workforce troubled him. Not only did nobody care about their jobs. The managers were worse.

Every place he could go, he had to earn respect. It was never given. A necessary reality I am sure. A solidly stupid one to Closet. He would work like no other. Once he had his respect he usually left. Now not all the times were of his own volition. Those times made it worse. Now he worked a job that paid enough to keep him afloat. The respect was there. He knew some fuck up of his lay around the corner. He loved his community and worked hard so they knew that. Every time it was not enough. Something always happened and it always was his fault. Always.

"I cannot fail."

Closet thought. He had positivity leaking around his life onto others. He loved life. Thankful for what was happening to him and for anything that would happen. Writing every day was rough. His coping mechanisms helped him feel more secure in this world. Safer in his thoughts. In getting his feelings out. Each time his pen pressed paper, Closet was further away from trauma. Whether undisclosed or not. It helped him stay off drugs. A problem he still had. Weed and alcohol prevailed through his daily time. His journal was an every day thing so far.

Reflected through this tale of Closet's life. A very easy life full of privilege. Privilege and prayer. Closet dealt with God as a loving creature. He knew no struggle he could not overcome. Especially after having his first therapist kill herself. He often wondered about who would have been his child. A heartbroken smile pierced his face through tears. What a world. To that he cracked open a beer. Beginning to drink through his emotions. He was not fully in control yet. Drinking for medicinal value. To slow his thoughts. When he drank he smoked. Sparking cigarette after another. Trying to make life different.

Closet chased emotional obscurity over clarity at the moment. He was privileged yet his life carried pain. He had a monkey on his back. Emotions to sift through. Some to keep. Some to let go. Staying sober was as closest to the goal as he wanted to get. As anything he could accomplish. It all started with one day at a time. Today was not that day. His tears flowed. He wailed. A deep sadness ate at his heart for the way he treated people. Not everything was his fault.

“Enough.”

He thought. He had to get his life together. One day at a time. He emptied out the beer into his mouth. His first and last one for the night. If you believed that, it was a lie. His parents did not need to hear he was gay anymore. They were happy that he was accepting himself. This ate at Closet. He had built his whole life around the fact of spite. He did not hate himself. He did not love himself as much as he could. Life was beautiful. Too beautiful. He felt he did not deserve the blessings he received. It was storming outside. Enough rain to hide his tears if he stepped out. He did not want them hidden. His emotions bare. No one was around anyways. No one could tell he was going through his shit. At least he thought.

His friends started noticing he was hanging out with them less. Drugs being the emotional ballast that held them down. He was trying to do different. Unsuccessfully. He just felt happier by his self. No one in his bed. He slept on the couch. As happy as he could be, Closet dealt with his problems every day. When life came at him anew, it was a new day. He felt this every day. Closet was surrounded with new opportunity. Most to better his life. Some to bring him down further. The latter being by his own hand. The former being blessings by God. A God he knew all too well. One that was loving and provided for their children. Everybody fit this definition. Closet believed that.

Closet also knew the devil. As he had felt them first hand just as everybody else in the world had. All except the purest of babies. Those who knew only pain. Pain misconstrued as love. A soul that never got the chance to rewind fast enough. That had to be the devil.

"Who knows?"

Thought Closet as he went into his beer once more. Thinking was all he could do in moments where his mind slipped. Better his mind than his hand. He knew death enough to know what would trigger it. A loose hand over looser lies as a loser did. Closet was a winner. Try convincing him that. He stood on no ground. Nothing he did as a man stood the test of questionable morals. A simple cigarette got him high. The same way his thoughts glowed he knew he could do better. The heat of his realization burned

Closet. What did he know that was not shown to him? A lot was the answer. One, he started to realize during this night of drinking. Not that he needed alcohol to pour over his thoughts.

He needed closure. Some of which he was not prepared for. At least at the time. Only time would tell. Time to his self-tended to be worse than hanging with his friends. They formed a support circle for him. A hard to find trait in life. A decent support circle. He hated being alone. He was even friends with his weed man. At least he thought so. You could never be too sure. With some of it figured out, life left Closet clueless. How many times could he bang his head against the same brick wall he was meant to climb? Only love prevailed when hate reared its righteous head against him. The drugs for sure did not help. A false positive for himself like depressions meds.

His emotions felt like the main problem for him. He always experienced them intensely. Even on slow days. Out they poured from excess. Only for others to see how he coped. Crying silently on every shoulder he would walk past that day. Figuratively until a soul offered him respite in a hug. He hated and loved himself at the same time. He was human. At least human enough. He had to remind himself. He loved life and life loved everybody.

Peace be with the fucks. Closet drove a hard bargain when he prayed. The hope he asked for not even the pope could ignore. Only his God could exist. No works against him would prosper. The peace this offered Closet was tenfold. He did not know how, but every day he got better. Increments at a time adding up. So simple yet promising was trying for… for his life. For others. He could not sell himself to the benefit of others. A lot of thinking through the alcohol.

He was hungry. In body and spirit. There was nothing that he believed he could not achieve. For anyone against him, Closet was a banana in their gun. Nobody could define him more than God. If he could just have his parents understand that. If he could have brought that to his therapist she might still be here. It was not his fault she killed herself. Anybody saying otherwise is selfish. Could he have saved her? That was a heavy weight on his shoulders. He could not be convinced otherwise. His new therapist helping him see past these impressions.

Closet's soul was getting tortured. He breathed the closure. It was beautiful. How someone could love him so much. They would not sleep with him. That respect was lost among Closet's locks. His features easily passable on a dating app. Much more so in person. He could laugh. He was easy to be taken advantage of. His opinion did not matter. Whoever slept with him had it in their mind to do so. Through means of alcohol or power.

Closet thought he was not anything special. Then again nothing mattered to himself except for his self. If only…if only. He needed to shower. He was swearing. He took his medicines. Closet cared. He did not know if he cared too little. All he knew was wishing others cared as much as he did. They did. Who was he to say they did not. Just a man in his own head. Never trapped. Solely ruminating. Like walking down a path by his footsteps.

He made it through. By the grace of God. A giving God. One who cared. One that did not require what he could not achieve. He was with a rewarding devil. One that benefitted him in pursuits of love. When he needed it and when he did not. He could not serve two masters. He would love one more than the other. At least that is what his book said. His book also showed him that only the shepherd can come to the sheep by the sound of his voice. Closet was a dogshit man. A dogshit person with a dogshit past.

Dogshit

His name was Dogshit. It fit him. Suited him better. Fit for his pedigree. Some would say he did not bat as high. yet to him it was easily misconstrued. Every drug every peso. Every penny. What did he not know of winning? Dogshit. Too simple a word for the self saboteur. His opinions none other than his self. The fact of the matter found through living. That it is a pile of Dogshit.

He wanted to fear himself. A neighborly guy. One filled with such sick regret. Where did they go as if they never left. His name was Dogshit. How did it compare to how he felt? Pretty valid. All which had been said a few lines before. Furthering his story, Dogshit started his day as he always did. Brushing his teeth. Time lost itself with the measure he took care of himself by. In his head he was stressed. Losing a part of his identity. He formed himself to fit with the plan. Yet there was barely one. He hated to see others cry over him. All he could remember. Tearing lives apart. He only wanted to heal.

His sexuality still ever present in his decision making. As much as he did not want it to be. It was. He could call his parents and let them know he might be gay. It did not matter anymore. They knew he dated dudes. That was enough. Enough for change. Maybe even a few dollars. Every bit of purchase was his.

Dogshit moved with the certainty of a general. Overconfident and incorrect. Never calm. His dog tag bearing the name he once called himself. Any name that could make him anybody. He prepared for the day as if he prepared for another wake. No one had died. He was just dramatic. To himself. Others around him did not see the amount of work that went into being Dogshit.

Anytime anyone got involved with the man himself he had something to prove. Otherwise, he was alone. Anyone connected to his name usually found out what it meant to be overshadowed. Outshined. Perplexing personification of his demons. A bottle was one of them. A blunt the other. Dogshit had everything to pour over did he not? His emotions. His life. A bottle of Listerine. His physical health important to him. It was a buffer to his emotions. He should start doing push ups.

Clever his mind. All he had to gain was fraught with trials. Wisdom. Fear especially. Love. How much could he want? The world. He wanted the world. It felt good to create. Unless it was despair. Then it felt great. He hated how much he loved himself. His drug problem more of an excuse next to his body count. He felt worse than he actually was. Dogshit.

He could sell you a story on why he was a victim. Did he buy it himself? He fell into his grief. A spring board for his better emotions. Today he was to hang out with his friends. He was excited. Something to drain the monotony of his emotions. Always whining. Dogshit was rarely in a beneficial mood. Solely displayed artificially to his companions. Today he meant it though.

His life needed the relief of pressure. Dogshit was to rebuild his life one step at a time. It was hard to. He owed it to his friends to better his life. Owed it to himself.

"I just wanted to be normal. Instead, I had to be fucking gay!"

"It's all bullshit in my head anyways."

"who's to say this is real… it is."

These were his thoughts. He thought about those kids in conversion therapy. He knew it never worked though. He would always be gay. Maybe he could be comfortable with it. It should not be such a big deal anyways. What the fuck. Did anything he cared about matter? To each his own.

Dogshit took a shower and readied to hang out with his friends. Today they would play board games. Some

DND. He needed the respite. His mind had been slow lately. A pace that suited him better. To achieve a base line normal was the goal however. His friends helped him achieve that. A nice release from the pressure of his life.

His new therapist helped him a considerable sum. Dogshit just wished he was more relatable. He sat as an authority figure. From the beginning Dogshit did not realize he would need to invest time. Time into this new person in his life. Maybe even to a point he would talk about his last therapist. Dogshit that is. Dog water this is. His heart was in it. All he could not believe in was in front of him. Love from his friends. He needed that.

These thoughts bounced out of his head as the shower rained on him. He needed this. He loved them. He knew they would never know him as his therapist did. Even then that was not love. It was…what was it? A necessity. Her life being lost along with his child bugged him. Every once in a while he would think of the bullet he dodged. She was a crazy bitch for that.

She did not love him. Not the way his mom and friends loved him. She was infatuated with who she thought he was. He was horny. Easily led. Dogshit stepped out of the shower and dried off. He got dressed. Brushed his teeth. These things were easy to keep up with now. He was getting better. His phone rang. Dogshit answered it to his best friend. They talked about meeting up.

Today they would be having a kickback at a mutual friend's house. Dogshit readied himself to be picked up. It was around this time that Dogshit began having lucid dreams. While he did not harm his friends, he emotionally abused his family in them. He used these dreams to let out manipulative behaviors. He did not know why he hurt his parents. He just knew it made him feel good. A deep pang of regret. Sunken into his chest. Then down into his stomach.

These dreams were frequent. He would need to talk to someone about them. His friends. His therapist. Someone.

He needed help. For now, he got that by hanging with his friends. They were here to pick him up. Going out the door and into the car, Dogshit was a passenger princess. Heading to his friends, he needed this. He was excited to get out of the house. Arriving at his buddy's abode, Dogshit promptly felt his anxiety slip away.

Knocking on the door they heard someone from inside the house calling them in. dapping up the tenants, dogshit grabbed himself a beer. Casually taking a sip he struck up a conversation in the group. They sat around a living room passing a blunt as time. He did not know if he should interject the time with his dreams. It was too nice right then. Beer atop tune they drank and listened to music.

The time came when they were all hungry. The house owner had cooked tacos. Dogshit's food sat warm in his belly. He loved his people. Tomorrow he would see his therapist. How would that go? He was not sure. No one could ever take the place of his last. An endearingly manipulative relationship. From both angles. He could not lie. He had time to fake the truth.

He stared into the void. One of his friends called out,

"Hey Dogshit!"

He turned to them with a smile. He could not register what they wanted at first. Then it hit him. They were motioning to the bathroom. Getting up Dogshit followed suit and made his way to the bathroom. Nose beers. Cocaine. They credited out lines on his friend's phone. Sniffing the snow, Dogshit felt excited. This was fun. Making their way back to the gathering they joined back in regularly.

This was a nice evening chilling with the homies. Dogshit eventually got up and went outside to smoke a cigarette. The one who drove him went out after him. Lighting a stogie, Dogshit conversed with his amigo.

"About what time do you wanna leave?"

"Whenever you want to go I'm down."

They took one last key to sober up and prepared to say their goodbyes. The host hugged them and told them she loved them. Driving home they chatted about the deeper pains in their lives. Dogshit opened up about his dreams. How he tore down his people. His friend told him maybe he should write about it. He did not know.

Dogshit brushed the idea off his shoulders. He was no writer. His friend told them they had started to sell blow. This was news to Dogshit. He assumed they had just bought a bag. Dogshit asked about the prices.

"Sixty a g."

Dogshit bought a bag. Arriving at his house they said their goodbyes and separated. Inside the house Dogshit cut up a line. He was going to pull an all nighter. Coke and video games did not sound so bad to him at the moment. As much as he had done for anyone in his life all came down to the little baggie of coke. This could fix even the most depressed day.

Dogshit knew his parents would be disappointed. If only he could see them as a family once again. He had been away for a while. He was mentally abusive to them. To those who held any close relationship with him. If he could just remember this when his therapist saw him the next day. A coked out appearance by Dogshit. He was living up to his name.

The next day came. Dogshit was sitting in his new therapist's office.

"Morning Dogshit."

"Morning sir."

“Have you put any thought into what you wanted to work on?”

“Yessir… I would like to talk about my dreams.”

“Your dreams?”

“Yessir, I dream lucid.”

“Okay.”

“Very lucid. I use it to mentally torture people.”

“Alright. Could you explain more?”

“It’s all people I know. I say the worst things to them. Do the worst to them.”

“When did this start?”

“Now that I think about it, I’m not sure.”

“This could be brought on by trauma, don’t you think?”

“That seems reasonable.”

“Do you see yourself as a bad person?”

“I see myself how I believe others see me.”

“Well, is that a yes or a no?”

“I don’t know. I hope not.”

Dogshit came to a conclusion that day. He was certain he could be a good person. Regardless of what others thought of him. However he would be made to seem doubtful in other’s eyes. He loved himself. A rare thought. How disappointing if the cup was half full. Except it was empty. He was ready to love himself. To let everything go. He was ready to pour his soul into his everyday. What a beauty that would be. His self love was abundant. If only to come across as cocky. In this day and age he was supposed to feel bad for having a dead baby and therapist. By his hand indirectly they died. Yet that was supposed to be in the past.

In truth, it ate at him. He could find no solace in his thoughts about her. So he chose to forget. To the best of his ability. He would be a piece of shit to be happy. She came to him in his dreams. Where he would swear and curse her. Say the worst things to her. Just to put her down. This was a guilty relief. How he blamed her for her own death. For the future that never would have been. Broken. She was broken like a dish. A dish smashed against the tile floor.

It was not his fault. He had to believe that. He thought that if he found somebody, he would be happier. That was a lie. A lie to himself and whoever he would be with. He had to hold himself accountable. So he was going to be happy. Besides, was it at the expense of others if she was already dead? Probably. That is why his name was Dogshit.

Life would take a turn for the unfortunate as Dogshit unable to keep a stable job lost his apartment. Bunny hopping from couch to couch his friends could not afford to house him any longer. They recommended he look into the homeless shelter. So he did. Still without a job, for lack of trying, he never did last at any sort of place. They were hoping that this would be a last step for him. A saving grace.

Taking a step out of the car Dogshit thanked his friend and walked to the entrance of the shelter. There they took his name down and told him to wait for a bed. It took a few hours but eventually he was assigned the top bunk in a corner near the back of a large room. The room was stuffed with multiple bunk beds. Enough to house 120 individuals. This was the male's dorm. Separate from the female dorm if only in location. Connected to the room was a bathroom filled with three shower stalls and three toilet stalls. There were four sinks lined up perpendicular to the stalls.

It was here Dogshit would rest his head at night for now. A lot awarded him within these walls. At the moment it was time to eat dinner. Dogshit waited in line. The food was wings. He would learn to appreciate them in the future. Today he was mildly disappointed in the quality of the food. Yet he ate still. After dinner they had chores to do. Taking out the trash being his. He grabbed two bags and proceeded to the dumpster.

"What the fuck is this place?"

He thought. Able bodied he got used to the routine with time. Compared to his old life this stage was depressing. A homeless shelter. He could not believe it. He wanted to do better. The days passed slowly. During daylight hours he was kicked out of the dorms to walk around the city. During his walks, Dogshit settled on the fact that he needed to keep a job. He needed money, some weed and to get out of this place.

Once on his feet again he would bust his ass to not lose his place. Asking around Dogshit discovered day labor. Some of the other residents let him know where to go and what to do. This work would pay ten dollars an hour. This was enough for him to start saving. The shelter was free. His money would be spent on weed and food. He set out to put aside 40 dollars in his savings a day. Easier said than done.

Food. The shelter's food was terrible. More than not Dogshit would get fast food. He kept spending money to eat.

He needed an EBT card. That would cut down on his purchases. He would live off of gas station food. He needed a ride. The day labor place had a van to take them to job sites. However, there was no vehicle to take him to his therapists or to the government building.

He would think about this while working. Formulating a plan while he picked up scrap on construction sites. Dogshit got paid the ten an hour to do construction site cleanup. It was not a bad gig. He would be up at around 6 a.m. Get dressed and by 7 he would be walking to the job works building. He would be accompanied by around five others each morning. Once there they would receive tickets. They were to hold onto these and return them signed at the end of the work day. Eighty dollars a day. Eight hours of work. They would then receive a check on return of the ticket signed. From there they would walk to the palm tree. There they could cash the checks. For a fee of course. They would end the day with 76 dollars in their pocket.

Where to save cash in front of homeless people without getting it stolen was turning into a predicament. He had a bank account but no way to get there except by foot. The credit union was across town. A one and a half hour walk. Guess he would start walking. He had to save the money every Friday after a full week's work. Dogshit would deposit one hundred in cash into his account. Not to be touched. He would get back on his feet. He did not have enough money some weeks to warrant the walk.

His saving was sporadic at best. Some days he would take a break and not go in. it was optional. On these days Dogshit would walk down to the corner store. Grabbing two forty ounces and a pack of darts. After, he met up with one of the dealers he befriended. He would hand him a forty and ten cash for two grams eyeballed.

They would then roll a blunt and smoke and drink on a park bench. These days were a treat to Dogshit. He had to learn to enjoy the smaller things. Being homeless in this life was teaching him that. He had a talk with his newfound buddy. Not about the upcoming politics. About what he thought of their lives. Not lacking for an answer, he responded kindly. In past lives he was a king. Now he spends his time around the corner store. Always ready with work.

This was not anybody's block. Just a block near the homeless shelter. Still his name was known. Always ready with a serve. Whether that be weed or crack. Sometimes ice got mixed in with the two. Usually with a few shards left in the bag of weed. Now whether this created new customers or not was yet to be found. Still, he loved dealing dope. The money was fast and made easily. He recounted the time he got shot to Dogshit.

"He had said something about my girl. So I stabbed him. Then, next thing I know, he's shot me in the leg."

The story was grueling rather than humorous. The reality of being on the street a dim one. As simple as broken into buildings. This life sucked. Was ass. Pure Dogshit.

Working cleanup was not pretty either. Dogshit recounted when he had to throw away human shit and piss. His buddy laughed. It was fucked. They would spend the whole day sitting there and laughing at the stories each told. It was a respite from the everyday.

"Custys" would come up and either buy weed or rock where they sat. Business was good. Finishing up their second blunt it was time for dinner. Dogshit got up and proceeded to walk back to the homeless shelter. It was spaghetti night. Something better than bones and rice. As he made his way back Dogshit formulated a plan to get his EBT card. He heard that there was a social services department at the shelter. Surely they could help him.

Finally back Dogshit walked through the front doors. Taking off his bookbag and items out of his pockets, Dogshit went through the metal detector. All clear. Picking up his stuff Dogshit passed through another door. Finally, he was inside the common area of the shelter. The line for dinner stretched from the main building out into the commons. There were hundreds of people here.

Dogshit would get into the progressively smaller line and wait. Eventually it was his turn to get a plate and a soda. Making his way back to the common areas, Dogshit found a seat. The food was bland but sustaining. He needed it to keep his energy. Tomorrow would be a construction site cleanup day. He had to save money to get out of here. This place was draining. Half the occupants were on some type of hard drug. Many getting suboxone scripts. This place was not for Dogshit. No matter how much he felt he deserved it.

His work ethic had picked up since he was there. Poverty inspired a change. He would bust his ass until he was finally out. Even if he was only saving around one hundred a week. He would need to lock in. He was to be here for a while. Dogshit finished his food and threw his plate in the trash. Walking to the dorm Dogshit got ready to go to sleep. He had to work tomorrow. The job was every day and any day. He could skip days if he wanted to. Like today.

He was determined to get out of this shelter. Right now, he needed it to keep him inside from the elements. Getting his clothes and towel ready Dogshit hopped in the shower. Cleaning himself he looked past the curtain that covered the stall. He saw eyes staring back at him.

“Hey! What the fuck?!”

Dogshit exclaimed. The eyes flew away as Dogshit put a towel around his waist and stepped out. The man was gone.

“Fucking perverts.”

He thought. Grabbing his clothes and stepping back into the stall Dogshit dried off and got dressed. Leaving the bathroom, he looked around the dorm. Some people were on their phones. Some reading books and eating snacks. He felt uncomfortable. Disliking the fact that someone had watched him in the shower. This place sucked.

Moving to the corner of the room Dogshit hopped into his bunk bed and got out his phone. These were the type of people to steal his shit and help him look for it he thought. He spent the rest of the night looking at memes as the clock ticked toward eleven pm. That is when Dogshit would go to sleep. Waking up tomorrow for a day of ten dollars an hour.

He dreamt he was talking to his unborn fetus. It had grown into a child. A little girl. She had no name. Was confused by it even. Feeling tears well up in his eyes he did not know why this was difficult.

"I know you didn't love mommy. That's why you'll never love me."

"What?"

Dogshit woke up in a sweat. His clothes were wet. The bed slightly damp.

"Fuck what time is it?"

He thought. Checking his phone, he saw it was 4:52 a.m. What a time to be awake. He laid in his bunk bed and checked his messages. Some of his friends had sent him memes over the night. Looking at them made him chuckle inside. He got up and dressed himself around 5:00 a.m. He walked out into the commons and smoked a cigarette. The shelter had prepackaged bag breakfast for the day laborers. Dogshit finished his stogie and got one. Some of the other patrons were up so he walked over to chat with some of them.

These were the same group of people almost every morning. Why they were still homeless was because nicotine, alcohol and drugs were expensive hobbies. Hobbies they all shared. They talked about which suburb they would clean today. Maybe it would be a parking garage? Some of them would smoke ice on the walk to the job works building. Dogshit preferred a blunt.

They left the shelter a little over an hour later and he rolled some green. Smoking as they all walked down the street. Marijuana was legal but ice or crystal meth was not.

Still, every start of the walk, a few of the workers would walk under some trees off to the side. The area blocked from the main road by bushes. There they would roll bowls and get high as hell. After, they would catch up to Dogshit's group and all walk to the day labor building.

The walk itself was around twenty minutes. They passed block after block. Shop after shop until the blunt was finally finished. Putting the roach into a cigarette pack they finally made it. There was a line outside the building of people who showed up to work. The day laborers were mostly homeless. They would put their money together for motels. Some else would sleep on the street. Others in the shelter.

If you added everyone's money together. The main items being bought were drugs. Ice, weed, dope of any kind. They waited in the line until 8:00 a.m. Doors opened and everyone was let inside. There, they all took seats until it was time for them to grab tickets. One by one a paper was passed around where they each wrote their names. Dogshit waited until it was his turn and put down his John Hancock. Passing the paper to the left of him he waited some more. Finally, his name was called out among others.

Getting up he collected his hard hat, tools and ticket. Once everything was in hand, Dogshit left in a van with around five other people. They would be going into a suburb development. Picking up the trash and items left behind. In the van they sat in relative silence. The drive was short about twenty minutes out of the way. Once there, they all got out and headed over to the big guy in charge. One by one they passed him their tickets. He broke down what they were to do.

Today was a new suburb they were building. Dogshit listened to the man while he sparked another morning cigarette. Once everyone was brought to speed, the boss left them to their own devices. He stayed in a trailer near the properties. Dogshit took the broom he brought with him and chose a house to sweep its outside. The ground was littered with nails, screws, bits of plastic and a plethora of other equipment.

There were people across the street speaking Spanish to each other. They were other workers who were not there as day laborers. Those people worked construction as a career. They were skilled most of all. Roofers, framers, etc. people who were not homeless. They for sure made more than ten dollars an hour. Dogshit had no idea what they were talking about.

"Fuckin immigrants amirite?"

A young man had walked up to Dogshit.

"What?"

"If you ask me they should learn English."

"I'm sure they do."

Responded Dogshit to the man. The young man continued on with idle chatter while Dogshit maneuvered a push broom around the driveway. He tried to ignore the man.

He just would not stop talking. Always with something to say about anyone Hispanic. The man was racist. Dogshit prayed to God for this man to go somewhere else. He could not bear to listen to his incessant bullshit anymore.

"Dude I'm trying to work."

This seemed to work as the guy left grumbling about how Dogshit wanted to be a Mexican. Dogshit could not stand people like that. Just dredging society. He just wanted to make his money and get the fuck out of there. He hated having to deal with drug addicts everywhere he looked. While he was judging them Dogshit was afraid he might become them. He would be 100% fucked then. His family would be done with him if he got hooked on ice. Right now, his parents worried about him. He was just too old to come stay with them. A fact he agreed on.

Sparking another cigarette the day passed on until it was noon. Time to eat. He had some cash on him. The Hispanics had set up a food truck that followed them to the jobsites. Dogshit went up to it and got a burrito and an energy drink for six bucks. Chowing down he swore on the quality of these mom-and-pop food trucks. His break was over as soon as he had started it.

With a broom in his hand walking to his destination, he had completed around four driveways so far. He just swept everything into a pile and threw it in the trash with a shovel. It was not bad work when the weather was pleasurable. It was brisk and chilly today in the morning. It warmed up near the afternoon.

Eventually it was time to meet back up at the trailer and collect their tickets from the boss man. Eight hours of work. Dogshit spotted his pay when handed his. That would be eighty dollars. He got in the van with his fellow day laborers. Once he turned in all his equipment borrowed and his ticket. He was handed a check from the front desk. He would walk to the palm trees to cash his check. It was only Monday. He would not be going to the bank today.

It was around 3:00 when Dogshit made it back to the shelter. He would eat the food they prepared him. They held onto food past dinner time for the day laborers. Today it was chicken wings. Not bad. He ate. When he was full, he smoked another cigarette and threw his plate in the trash. A ritual for him. He had been smoking more cigarettes as a homeless person. There was just not much to do. He could not jerk off because there was no privacy. He had to work. All he could do was play on his phone or read a book.

Lights out was at ten p.m. Memes. Every night it was memes that he would fall asleep to. They reminded him of a simpler time. Before everyone around him smoked meth. Lulled to sleep by the light of his phone, Dogshit would do it all again tomorrow. This was his schedule for months. He would work until he could afford a deposit on an apartment. Saving one day out of the week to hang on the corner with his dealer. He was about halfway to a thousand when he discovered the shelter had a social services program.

Checking it out he found they had applications for EBT and section 8.

"Wow!"

This blew his mind. These programs could not have been effective he thought. There were too many homeless people. Dogshit noticed there were two types of homeless. Those addicted to hard and those who were not. Himself being the latter. He swore to himself he would make it out of here. So, on a Monday morning Dogshit did not go to work. He woke up, showered and brushed his teeth. Left the dorms and went to the main building connected to the commons.

There sat a woman and a man at a desk. Behind them was the cafeteria and TV area. Dogshit walked up to the desk.

"Hello, I would like to schedule an appointment with the social services."

"Okay, and what's your name?"

The lady asked.

"Dogshit."

He replied.

"Okay, Dogshit, we'll get that scheduled for you."

"Sweet!"

He thought. A little help to escape this hole was fine by him. Skipping work to get this done probably put him ahead in life a few steps. Work smarter, not harder. Still he had to work his way out of being homeless. Which rain or shine is what he planned to do. Intentions were everything behind his work ethic. For the right cause, he would break his back. Now he just had to bide his time. Eventually he would be gone from this place.

"Okay Dogshit. Your appointment is tomorrow at 9:30 a.m. Can you handle that?"

Dogshit snapped back to reality. He needed a cigarette.

"Yes ma'am. I appreciate you."

"You're welcome sweetie."

What the hell? Why Was he a sweetie? Oh well at least he would be further ahead tomorrow. With that he walked out of the main building. He passed through the commons as he left out the front building. Guess he was missing another day of work. He sparked a stogie. He decided he would check on his dealer. Even though they hung the other day.

Walking to the corner Dogshit looked around. This city was growing. The amount of homeless, him included, was insane. Everywhere he looked he saw a need for change. Hopefully this appointment went as he needed. He barely knew a thing about government assistance. His parents had provided everything for him growing up. He had wants of course but all his needs were met. Now he was thrust into a world constantly getting realer. Food was on a timeline and scarce. He had not seen his therapist since he became homeless. All Dogshit could think about was smoking weed and hanging.

Day labor sucked and was inconsistent. He got paid a half day for having fell asleep on the job. He should not have smoked that blunt during lunch he thought. He needed to get on his feet again. He knew it somehow involved the human resources at the shelter. Some found reliance on the state embarrassing. Dogshit merely thought of surviving. If there was a way to game the system, he would find it. He was just an average homeless person. Extremely under appreciated. Those who could not relate to the struggle looked at those in the circus with disdain. They were better than the homeless. Anybody was in their mind inferior. No explanation needed. It was a way of life.

Who could predict what one homeless man could achieve? A normal life? He was pulling ahead of what these bastards thought of him. Can he do it? He wondered. A thought used to spite himself. Of course he could do it. God loved him and provided this opportunity. He had faith he would be accepted. He turned in an application and two weeks later, he got the news. Declined.

What did he do to deserve this. Not enough apparently. If only he had done more. What could he have done? Exasperated he sat down on a bench. It was in the shelter's common area. He looked to his right and saw a baggie on the bench next to him. It was filled with what looked like glass. This baggie turned out to be what is known as ice cream, ice, aka meth. He was sick of this shit. How could he stay away from drugs when they fell in his lap. This was bullshit.

Dogshit took the meth and threw it in the trash. He thought about this for around five seconds. He jumped into the trash can and fished the baggie out. This was money. He would be stupid to throw it away. Now he had a soggy bag of meth. He stuffed the bag into a cigarette pack and ran into his dorm. Sliding into the bathroom Dogshit cracked out his phone. Dropped a few crystals in a piece of paper, crushed it then laid out a line on his cellular. Rolling the paper up he then snorted the line.

Dogshit realized, like everyone, he liked meth. Life was not fair however. Many people were. This was eighty dollars in his hand if he played his cards right. A full day's work. He knew just the people to sell it to as well. Two young men that had talked to him earlier. He wanted to offload it to them. Yet, they convinced him to do it with them.

The ice lasted them a week. Budgeting how much they would take by smoking it out of glass bowls. They would crush it up in paper and snort it as well. Anything short of drinking their own piss. Which was a way to get high mind you. That and needles. Dogshit could not do needles. He did not wish to die.

Dogshit laid on his bed in the dorm. The bag of work in his pants. Him and a few others binged for days. Getting high. He did not sell a single piece of dope. He was a terrible drug dealer. Getting high off his own supply. Who was he to even compare himself to those doing better than him. Shit sucked like a glass dick. Dogshit was in love with illicit substances.

Dogshit finished the bag on a new day. He had done most of it with his roommates. He wanted more. He figured he could talk to his dealer about getting some. Meth sold like candy. People wanted it. He could just hang out with his homeless friends. They would buy it off him throughout the night. All the while they all smoked it. Sometimes they snorted it. Crushing it in between a piece of paper.

One night in the park, they got caught. Dogshit had been smoking with his friends and had his bag on him. He had a felony on his person. The cop searched him and found the bag in his underwear. He and all his friends got arrested. They had no money to post bail. Dogshit had failed to save what little money he had. They spent the night in holding.

Their paraphernalia was confiscated, including a glass bowl. He most of all was cooked.

He did not get the same treatment as the others. They were out in the morning. Dogshit used his one phone fall to call his parents the next day. In less than 24 hours Dogshit's parents had bailed him out. They took him to their house. They said he could stay if he stopped fucking up. He agreed and put ice behind him. Those were his old ways. That did not mean he put weed and cocaine up for good.

His court date was set a few months down the line. His parents said they would get him a lawyer. How lucky was the loather? He felt estranged with his parents. His sexuality burdening him. He was bisexual. That was all he could convey to his parents. They suggested he should resume therapy. Dogshit agreed. He knew he still needed help. His days on the street had changed him. As did the drug use. Dogshit was constantly paranoid. He would think others were gang stalking him. He had a lot to recover.

Living with his parents he felt like a child again. The only way he could explain it was a lack of responsibility. Mom and pop would cover it. He was at home base again. They loved him. More than he could comprehend. A feeling he did not want explained. Only if he could stop doing drugs. Would that not be cute for the family? All perfect. His parents could not know the full extent. He said it was only alcohol which was a lie. Then he said it was only weed. A lie again. Even though they were both legal, his parents wanted him sober.

He needed a job. He needed direction. For that they believed he had to be sober. What a queer thought for a queer guy. Who held hope as no other. Hope he would be, he could be normal. His best friend had been his drug dealer. He lost that relationship when he moved in with his parents. They were keen for him to go back to school. What for, he had no idea. Probably business. That seemed simple enough.

He still smoked pot every day. A habit they hated to see formed. They tried many ways to get him to stop. However, Dogshit just would not listen. Oh well, was the consensus. At least it was not ice. His relationship with his parents grew stronger as he stayed with them. All talks about his sexuality were kept to a minimum. His parents did not care as much as he thought they did. He was glad for that.

They even talked about putting him back in therapy as he did not have a therapist while homeless. He barely knew his last one. All in due time he would have his life back. He may not have his own place. Yet, he had a loving and caring family. He could never had imagined that he would be back with his parents. Still this show of love was more than he could ask for. He was grateful. His life had hit bumps. Still, it was changed for the better.

They suggested he get a pet. Something to relate to as he was rebuilding his life. He was not estranged to the idea and agreed. This was all fine to Dogshit. Yet he still had his court case for the drugs. That day would come and go. With Dogshit receiving probation for two years. He was not able to receive pretrial intervention as he had a weed charge from when he was eighteen. This put a stop to him smoking weed. Indefinitely. The animal Dogshit chose to get was a cat. An all white cat he named Aurelius.

Aurelius was a cuddly cat. One that kept Dogshit company. His parents were right. He could not blame them for him getting more responsibility with a pet. It was something he did not know he needed. His life was being saved by the two people he hated all his life and a furball he found at the shelter. Basically thrown in the trash. Aurelius was not trash to him however. Not to say he bonded to the cat immediately. At first he could have cared less about the cat.

One day the bastard rubbed up to Dogshit when he was crying. This opened the door for Dogshit realizing animals had empathy. After that, Aurelius was a king among men and felines. Dogshit would cuddle and hold his cat every day it felt like. His parents were happy to see his love for the cat. They were worried about their son. His closeted sexuality had just come into bloom when he told them he was bisexual. They loved him. They just wanted him to be true to his self.

This was still seeming a lot to ask. As new as his title of Dogshit perused self hatred. It was not that he hated himself. It was that his title mocked his actions. As for later he was indeed a piece of Dogshit. The worst was yet to pass. What the ice had started, Dogshit would thirst. He started having bouts of psychosis. His cat Aurelius was a saving grace for him. He felt like he had a new best friend.

Barely any of his friends checked in on him while he was homeless. Oh well. All he needed was his family and his cat. His therapist was also a help. Dogshit's parents were getting him back on track. However, the psychosis had seeped into his brain and planted a seed. A seed of doubt, paranoia and fear. It would present itself over the course of his stay with his parents. Small signs. His name being called every so often. Other thoughts entered Dogshit's head he felt were not his. Minor things, like stick his hand in the garbage disposal. Which he would not do. Just weird he thought it.

Laying in bed Dogshit heard his name get called outside his room. Ignoring it he thought nothing of it. A few minutes later he heard.

"Dogshit I know you heard me."

Well, he mainly felt the message. Disturbed he walked to his closed door and opened it. Half expecting someone to be on the other side. Dogshit was surprised and relieved just to see Aurelius at the door mewing.

"Oh thank god."

"Finally."

The cat responded.

"Yikes!"

Exclaimed Dogshit.

"What the fuck!?"

He swore he just heard his cat talk. He did not hear it physically. In his head the thought bloomed into existence. Looking at Aurelius the cat only replied with a mew. He walked into Dogshit's room and hopped on the bed. Dogshit's head was silent. Closing the door he went to his bed and sat down. Aurelius walked up to him and head butted his thigh. Petting his cat Dogshit felt loved more than any other. He fed him.

Aurelius relieved Dogshit's paranoia. Among other things. It was a mutually beneficial relationship. Does an animal know love? Who knows on that front? However, Dogshit was comforted by the presence of his therapy cat. All he needed was a letter from his therapist. That validated his need for the cat. Dogshit was in love. He had an adorable little buddy. One who he could talk to. All Aurelius would do is listen.

"Hello little guy."

Dogshit said to the cat lifting him up into his arms. petting Aurelius' cheek with his fore finger and thumb, the cat purred. A nice throaty grumble from his favorite little guy. This was a nice release for Dogshit. Again he heard a voice in his head of the cat.

"They're coming for you."

"What the fuck i'm trippin!"

Dogshit exclaimed. He had received a text a few days ago that a friend thought he was dead. Now his cat is talking to him? He was struck with fear to the core. This was not going to end well. As Dogshit took a deep breath, he grabbed his pill bottle and popped an anxiety med. This had become a common habit for him if he could not deal with the real world he would pop a pill.

"Hurt the infidels."

He heard. He could only describe this sensation as the closest thing to telepathy. With his cat. Aurelius.

Now of all times for this to happen, might have been because his exposure to ice in his weed. Ice in his ice. Drug induced psychosis. Had to be it. Otherwise the government is inducing psychosis in Dogshit. The closest way to defer information was perceived through his cat. The now still silent cat. his intuition that the cat was right stuck with him. He had no one if he did not have his parents. As Dogshit thought that he received thoughts from Aurelius again.

"Your parents were murdered."

"Shut the fuck up!"

He exclaimed as he dropped the cat. Crying he curled in a ball on his bed.

"It can't be true."

He mused to himself over and over. This had broke his psyche. He just wanted to go to sleep so he did. Maybe life would be better when he woke up. Maybe he would not have a psychotic telepathic cat. This was not assured. His life was crashing down again. He did not know what to do. So he slept. Dogshit awoke to his mom telling him it was time for dinner. He got out of bed and walked to the kitchen. Aurelius was sitting on the foot of his bed. Silent as a normal cat would be. Giving his mother a hug Dogshit sat down at the dining room table. It was there he noticed that something was different about his parents. They seemed weird. His cat assured him these people could not be his parents.

"How is it honey?"

His mom asked. Dogshit was freaking out. His parents were not his. He got up and excused himself from dinner. Rushing to his room he locked the door. Aurelius was still on the bed.

"I need you to talk."

Dogshit pressed. The cat remained silent.

"Fuck."

Was Dogshit's only thought. His paranoia ate at him. He was sure his family was changed. He would start to look at them more closely. At least his cat was there to comfort him. Aurelius. The one he started to depend on with his psychosis from drug use. This would be the turning point for the family. Dogshit suspecting his parents' lives had been replaced. This was next level.

He could not imagine such a world. So he cried. Pouring tears into his pillow. Nothing could bother him anymore. His cat in his head. Talking to him. He picked up Aurelius and cuddled him. His cat a comfort in his paranoia. Brushing the cat's fur back Dogshit gave him five kisses on the nape of his neck. He was worried. He had to check on his parents. He wished to see how different their replacements were. His blatant trust in his animal was all he had left.

Resigned to check on his parents later, Dogshit turned on the tv in his room. His paranoia falling as he watched cartoons. His mind was fried. Crying it out helped. Still, Dogshit's life was falling apart. He fell asleep. His dreams were purveyed with a lucidness. His cat, Aurelius, a constant. Unbeknownst to him, he would become a murderer. Of who?

Well just find out. His life flashing before his eyes. A depressing sentiment. Such a pleasure this cat brought. Nothing could compare to what he was feeling.

A sigh breathed across his chest. Tired. He was tired while sleeping. What he wished one could only imagine. A pain only he suffered burned between his eyes. A need like no other. His mind a bullet point of anxiety. His life viewed from an outside perspective. What an easy sight to behold. Dogshit awoke to his mom knocking at his door to ask if he was alright. He could not ignore her. Piping up, he answered her.

"Honey, can you unlock this door?"

He got up and proceeded to the door. Unlocking and opening it he sat face to face with the imposter mother. Small things about her were different. The fullness of her cheeks. The part in her hair. Dogshit knew this was not his mother.

"What do you want?"

"You just seem off honey. Is everything okay?"

Dismissing her Dogshit did not want to talk to the imposter further. He had seen enough. Shrugging her qualms away, Dogshit closed the door. The government was in on this. He knew it. He looked at Aurelius. Half expecting him to talk. He was going crazy. He knew that for sure. Dismissing his imposter mother clearly bothered her. What did he care? His real parents were dead. He could see the subtle changes in the imposters. He hoped they did not catch on that he had.

His father would be the same as his mother. A crude fake. Crying. He started to cry again. His life was close to over. He hated this. Cuddling Aurelius, Dogshit cried himself back to sleep. This was his day. A sad fortune presented to the man. He missed his parents. He wished they did not get killed and replaced. The world was taunting him. Slowly he was failing to meet his goal of normal. Normalcy. They were coming after him.

The conspiracy ran deep through his spine. He knew what he had to do. Could he do it? He was eating shit from the hands that fed him. This was no simulation. Dogshit really could die at any moment. He froze in fear. His time was running out. This weighed on him heavy. He left his room and went into the kitchen. His parents were asleep in their room. Grabbing a butcher knife from the stand, Dogshit stepped into his parents' room. If it was not for the government Dogshit would not be Dogshit.

His imposter mom awoke from him entering. He stabbed her first. Lunging towards her, he buried the knife into her chest. He proceeded to do that three more times before his father tackled him. Swinging punches to Dogshit's head. During the struggle they both got knocked down. The knife finding it into his imposter father's lung. Turning to lay on his side Dogshit's fake dad asked him nothing as he struggled to breathe.

Dogshit got up and went into the bathroom. Going to the toilet he took off its basin lid. Walking back into the connected bedroom he stood over the man sent to replace the patriarch of the family. Raising the lid, Dogshit rained blows down to his imposter father's head. Wave upon wave crashed into the man Dogshit never knew. Looking over at what he had done. He felt a sense of relief from his demons. He could not go on the run. Besides, the government was testing him. They would not want to throw away a good experiment before the results.

Dogshit called the cops to turn himself in. The phone call was short. Dogshit was brief and pointed. Enunciating clearly. Multiple squad cars were sent to check in on the damage. Once there, they saw dogshit sitting on the porch smoking a cigarette. Covered in blood. Addressing him they drew their weapons. Drawing closer to the man he offered no resistance. He went peacefully in cuffs. No suicide by cop.

Dogshit's mind as innocent as a baby's. In the back of the patrol car, he saw the police enter the house. The damage they saw looked too surreal to be faked. A man laid on the ground. His skull caved in. Bubble gum like bits of brain littered the top of his corpse. As well as a few feet away. The woman laid on the bed. Her night gown stained with blood.

The lid to a toilet tank sat upon the floor. It too was covered in blood.

"What the fuck?"

One of the officers said. Walking back outside they called for crime scene to get there. It was a lot to take in. they could not believe Dogshit's story when he told it. Could not fathom the depths his mind took him to. He was crazy. He was not injured except for a bruise on his eye. Once EMS got there the blood had already dried around the strangers Dogshit killed. As well as on himself.

He was to stay hand cuffed in the back of the police cruiser. Other than that, he caused minimal to no problems.

After his fake folks were checked, they drove Dogshit to the police interrogation room. There he was to be questioned. Fed as well. Primarily talked to to gain an insight into these grisly murders.

"Do you like food?"

"Everybody likes food."

Started one of the officers.

"Yea I'll take A burger and fries meal."

Dogshit replied.

"Anywhere in particular?"

"There's a place near Cicada East high that should be open."

"Okay we're gonna get you that food. For now, why don't you get comfortable in that chair? Answer a few questions."

"That's fine with me."

The interrogation had just started when Dogshit received his burger order. Paying more attention to the food rather than the officers. Dogshit answered questions with indiscretion. He was honest and upfront with them. His parents were not his actual parents. They were plants from the government. These people were gang stalkers and after him. Yea. They thought for sure they got a crazy one in that night.

Dogshit admitted to everything. He was for sure going to get locked up with the key thrown down a drain.

"Damn, so those were not your real parents?"

"No sir. They were look alikes sent for I don't know what. They weren't my real parents."

That line and many more would get brought up in his court case. His public defender pleading for insanity. No family visited him while he was in prison awaiting his sentence. They hated him. He had taken from them a whole two lives. Those were hard to come by. Especially for ones you love. There would be no match for the memories they shared. For all they knew, he never shed a tear for those lost. He was dirty. Worse than scum. He was Dogshit.

His trial came and went. He was found guilty of two counts of second degree murder. As he had not planned to kill his parents. He just did. He was to be sentenced to life in mental hospice. His lawyers getting the jury to lean towards insanity. He showed no remorse, just confusion at what he had done. This cannot be real. They were imposters! Now he is spending life in a mental institution. It was a plea deal and Dogshit did not know how he would fare in prison. Damn. The whole world was against him.

His new life. One of constant boredom. Adjustment was minimal. He would wake up. Take his meds. Then he would eat breakfast alone in his room. Surrounded by five walls. Five white walls. His day was that of routine. Wake up, eat, group activities, eat more, more groups, repeat. Dogshit was going insane. More so than he already was.

He took his time to write while in the asylum. Spending what free time he had keeping a journal. This would prove to be beneficial to his self care. Dogshit hated it here. His days were empty.

"I'm going to be here forever."

Dogshit thought.

One day he saw a girl crouching down and picking up things in the corner of the outside area. Curious Dogshit walked over to see what she was doing. From afar he could not tell. As he got closer, he realized she was digging in an ant hill. She would clear some of it away. Stick her fingers in it and grab one. Then proceed to let it bite her.

After letting her do this a few times Dogshit walked up to her.

"You shouldn't hurt yourself like that."

He said.

"Oh no, it doesn't hurt. I just like popping the bumps."

"The what?"

"You know, the bumps ants make when they sting you."

"But why?"

"I don't know. I just do. Don't you think as creatures we should just exist?"

"Not without a purpose. What's life without."

"Well, what's your purpose?"

"To get the people that murdered my family."

"I'm sorry."

"It's fine."

"What's your name?"

"My name is Dogshit."

"Well hello Dogshit. nice to meet you!"

"You too."

They would soon talk to each other almost every day. Aside from personal space they were rarely seen without each other. Dogshit and the lady he made his friend. They taught each other. Read the same books. The two were a mirror of each other. Except one had a penis. The other a clitoris. When one was upset the other calmed them down. When one was watching the door, the other showered. These two were inseparable.

It was only eventually that a bump formed in the woman's stomach. A bump like no other. They knew that the doctors would not let them keep it. As soon as it was noticed she was put on watch. Which did not make sense to the parents. You could not get pregnant at the same time twice. Nevertheless, they offered her the chance to get an abortion. One which she refused

They both wanted to keep the baby. Even if they could not keep the baby. Life was strange. This was the worst. How was he supposed to change the world if he could not keep his seed? Who would raise it? Too terrible to avoid. Her problems were his problems. He wanted the baby as much as she did. The hospital thought otherwise. Two patients could not be parents. Dogshit and his new love. Boths opinions discounted. They did not matter to the state. He needed to calm down. So Dogshit and the girl that associated with him listened to music during therapy.

"What the fuck was going on?"

She thought. Dogshit told her he had a plan to escape. Escape this routine of forced normality. As if. He often wondered how Aurelius was doing. He missed his cat. Now he had to come up with a plan to escape this hell. This day he had a meeting with the staff psychiatrist. The last thing he wanted to talk about was his lady. Figured this would be the first topic she brought up.

"So how are you and the other patient doing?"

"Fine."

Dogshit responded unkindly. He was tired of the bullshit. The ins and outs of the healthcare system was total bullshit. Hell, the staff often ate the spare trays. They could save them for the patients. Many minor things such as that bothered Dogshit. He saw problems everywhere he looked. It was draining. On the staff and himself.

"Too bad."

He thought. The sentiment carried by both sides. Who deserved this? Was anything purposeful? Or did each day pass inhibited by their minds? What they thought was right. For fucks sake he had not had a beer in forever. He missed the daily nuances he dealt with outside of the hospital.

"Dogshit."

His psychiatrist voice dug him out of his stupor.

"Dogshit. do you feel like you want to harm yourself or others?"

"No."

He replied.

"Have you ever wanted to?"

"At times yes. Woe is me I guess."

"Okay."

The conversation was lacking. He was just here to get on a new anxiety medication. Hopefully something stronger. With that the meeting came to a close. Dogshit was escorted out of the office. Into the common area. Metting up with his two babies, he gave them a hug. The soon to be mother pursed her lips and pressed them against his. Mwah. What a gal! was it love or just ignorance that kept them together? She knew he was a killer. Yet, she still chose to be near him throughout the day. Such a simple yet provocative couple. They were both human none the less. What more could they wish for? They wanted freedom but had each other. What else could they do but therapy and themselves. Not anymore as she was on watch.

Dogshit's hatred of the system grew. They were supposed to help him. Instead, they exacerbated his symptoms. Made him feel a rage against the machine. He could groan and sigh as much as he wanted to… nothing changed. At the end of the day nobody could tell Dogshit he was wrong. He would only listen to himself. Not even his girlfriend.

One day Dogshit woke up ready to be as difficult a patient he could be. The only one to calm him down was his lady. He could not have her stressed while pregnant. Shit, he even quit smoking cigarettes to support her morally. They were a team. Combating boredom with conversation, games, and each other's lips. The time would pass. The day to give birth and relinquish the baby was nigh. They hated what they were forced to do. Without even a name, their child was taken into the system. Where was the justice? No one would have loved their baby more than them. Distraught and heart broken, the mom laid back down on her hospital bed. After a day or two the doctors let her back into the ward.

Immediately when they saw each other Dogshit and her embraced. Through tears they sobbed quietly. Heart broken for their future.

"It's okay. It's gonna be okay."

Dogshit told her. The two let go and proceeded to sit down on a bench in the outside common area.

"Well, this means we can smoke cigs again."

Dogshit said to his partner. She did not find it funny. With a sigh, she dug into dogshit.

"You know, I wish you never got me pregnant."

"We can't change anything."

He said.

"You think you're always right huh? You couldn't even give me a whole day to grieve before you started cracking jokes."

She was pissed. Dogshit sat in silence for some time. Not knowing how to respond. He did not want to seem shallow or manipulative. Two traits he hated about himself. He was a selfish man. A creature of habit. One too caught up in his own shit to even smell others. She was hurting. All he did was make it worse. What could he do? What could he say? He was at a loss for words. All he wanted to do was show he cared. All he did was make things worse.

"Well what do you want me to do?"

He asked.

"I just want you to try God dammit!"

With that she got up and left him. Alone at the bench. Walking up to the attendant, Dogshit asked for a cigarette. They complied and passed him a menthol 100. Taking a long drag Dogshit thought about his plan to escape. How it would mean nothing without her. Once finished, he put the cigarette out on his palm. Sighing with the pain. As he exhaled he prayed to his God. If he ever needed them, now was the time.

He wondered about his cat Aurelius. How he had convinced him his parents were imposters. What happened to that little deity? He missed him. The cat would surely know what to say to him in times like this. For now, Dogshit was alone. Depressed by himself. He wondered if his girlfriend just broke it off with him. Sure seemed like it. What would he do? Surely God would not abandon him like this. He was so certain he was a soldier of the lord. All that was was psychosis.

Dogshit had gone crazy. As he laid on his bed ready for the nightly check, he prayed. Prayed for a sign to come to him. Did anything he did matter? He was stripped of everything. Doomed to stay here for the rest of his life.

A tech walked into his room. Wrote on a notepad, then left. Dogshit was too tired. He needed rest. So he fell asleep. He would get checked on throughout the night. Every 15 minutes exactly. Not that he cared, his life was forever put on hold. Something he could not change. As the days passed Dogshit's ex ignored him. He would try and sit his tray next to her. She would get up and walk away. He felt downtrodden. He missed his love.

She held all the power. Dogshit would begin putting more and more cigarettes out on his hand. He could not take the agony. Weeks passed. Finally, Dogshit resolved to take his own life. He would overdose. Dogshit had been requesting Ativan and hiding it in his room after fooling the nurses. He also fermented some orange juice from the cafeteria. He was to make a cocktail that would put him to sleep. Never to wake up. Benzos and alcohol. A deadly combination.

The night came when he was to do it. Sitting on his bed, the ward went into lights out. Dogshit had saved 30 Ativan and about 15 ounces of fermented orange juice. The tech walked into his room. Checked on him and left. Dogshit had 15 minutes. Now was the time. Swallowing all his pills and downing the hooch. Dogshit became inebriated with shallow breathing. The edges of his vision started to blur. As he felt himself slipping away, he heard footsteps. Shit a tech. the foot steps drew nearer until Dogshit could feel the man's breath on his ear. The man spoke.

"It's all over now Dogshit. you served your purpose."

Dogshit remained silent. He was inebriated and barely breathing but still alive.

"We tested you. The homelessness. The miscarriage. Your parents' deaths. All us. We killed your parents. Nice job spotting their replacements."

With that Dogshit inhaled deeply and lunged at the tech. his barred out hands around the man's neck. Choking him.

"You fuugin bastard!"

Punching him in the ribs the tech fought back.

"I wannn answersss!"

Dogshit yelled while banging the techs head onto the floor. Dogshit heard more footsteps. He looked up to see the nurses and other techs standing outside his door. They were silently watching as he killed one of their own. What the fuck was going on? The tech went limp scratching at Dogshit's face… arms collapsing, he was dead. Dogshit would not be getting answers from him anytime soon.

After the ordeal was over, the nurses proceeded to walk into the room.

"Ssstay Baack!"

Dogshit shouted as he got up and scooted his self into a corner in a stupor. His words slurring. His vision grew darker as he fell to the ground. The last thing he saw was the other hospital staff dragging the dead techs body away. "What was happening?" He thought as he slipped into darkness.

Solemn

I awoke strapped to a table. I groggily came to enough to get aware of my surroundings. I did not know where I was. Only who I was. Someone of little value. My last memories were a blur. I had swallowed around 20 plus pills. Alcohol with it as well. How was I not dead? Again, where was I? A man walked into the room from the door in front of me. Next to it was a large mirror. Probably double sided. The man spoke.

"Hello, I am Doctor Whittaker."

"Who?"

I responded.

"The doctor responsible for you here. You see as a child, a chip was implanted into your brain. Right through your soft spot."

"What the fuck are you talking about? Where am I?"

"Every minor hallucination. Those voices in your head. All controlled by us."

"But why?"

I was confused

"Well, we were hoping to turn you into a killer. Little government experiment."

"I don't believe you."

This Dr. Whittaker was full of shit.

"Oh no?"

The Dr then pressed a button on a remote he held and spoke into it. The voice that came out into my head was of my cat Aurelius. What the fuck.

"You see, all controlled by us. Everything you did was to help our study. We wanted to see if we could control a person through psychosis. According to the data I'd say we were successful."

"But what about my parents?"

"They signed you up for this program. They're long dead, but they knew the risks. They wanted to tell you. So we killed them. Replaced them, with lookalikes."

I could not believe this. Anger and hatred bubbled at my strapped down chest. I despised this man and the people he worked for.

"Fuck you!"

I spat at him.

"You know, your parents wanting you to be a homosexual was a part of it too."

I repeated the last sentiment. I needed to get out of here. It looked like that plan was fucked at the moment. I hated it here. I strained against the restraints. They were strapped down tightly.

"What do you want from me?"

"Well now that we've turned you into a killer we can control, you have two choices. The first, you do what we tell you and we let you free. Or we put you down like a failed lab rat. The choice is yours."

I did not know what to think. I did not want to die. Working for the people that killed my parents however was down right deplorable.

“Well to be fair they signed up for it.”

Fuck, he could read my thoughts. What was this?

“Oh it’s just the chip don’t worry.”

Fuck.

“Okay I’ll listen to you but I want to see my kid.”

“Well, here’s the thing. Your kid does not exist.”

“What do you mean? I clearly knocked somebody up in the hospital!”

“All faked. Your girlfriend was never pregnant.”

This Dr. Whittaker was a real piece of shit. I hated him. Yet I did not want to die. With a sigh I conceded.

“Good. Now all you have to do is listen to that little voice in your head.”

Slowly my vision started to darken again. I tried to fight it but ended up asleep. I wanted answers. Maybe this was the way?

I awoke again. This time on a street corner with people passing over me. I was fully clothed in a city I did not know. Standing up I began to walk. I had to figure out where I was. A voice in my head piqued up.

"Check your pocket."

In my pocket was a piece of paper. It had an address on it. My other pocket a phone. I knew where I had to go. I put the address into maps and proceeded to my destination. I fucking hated these people. A man's got to live however. I was not stronger than a whole structured entity. Whatever this was. I would find out.

The apartment was a few blocks down from where I woke up. All this walking was hurting my liver. It probably was me recovering from the pills. I turned a corner and bam. There it was. The Cicada apartment complex. I walked up to the gate and pressed the buzzer on a post out front. The gate opened. The paper said go to 105 so that is where I headed. First floor I thought. Finally I had found apartment 105 a voice in my head told me to knock five times in a specific pattern. Knock knock knock…knock knock

“Good.”

It told me.

The door opened up and a man stuck his head out. He asked for my name. which I gave him. Then he let me in. The place was quaint with a living room that connected to a kitchen. Two bedrooms and one man standing in the center of it all. He told me to go in the second room towards the back. So I did. The voice in my head told me to open the door. So I did. Inside the room was a blind folded man tied to a chair. Next to him was a table with a gun.

The entire floor of the room was covered in plastic. The voice in my head told me I was here to kill the man. To pick up the gun. Shoot him in the head. The man hearing me walk in started to beg for his life. It did nothing. He knew nothing. Why was he here? All questions I had myself.

"Please!"

He begged and begged. I could do nothing to help this man. I picked up the semi automatic pistol. Pointed it at his head and pulled the trigger. Click! The gun was not loaded. Crying uncontrollably the man pleaded with me. The voice in my head told me I was done and to leave the complex. On the way out the voice told me to check my back pocket. In it was a wallet. It had an ID and a credit card in it.

"You can use this money as you see fit. As long as you do what we say. Failure to oblige will result in death."

Damn. They were not kidding. I had no idea why the gun was empty. I did not know who that man was or what he did. Yet I did not hesitate to pull the trigger. Who was I? I was becoming a monster. I could feel it. Yet without much of a choice. I walked to a local restaurant and sat down. I did not know how much money was on the card. I had to hope it was enough. It was.

This routine went on. I was asked to the apartment. Walked into a room to see a different man tied to the chair. There was always a gun on the table. The gun was always empty. The people I held a gun to always begged for their lives. I got used to the crying. The begging. I did not know what happened to the men after. All I knew was that I was getting paid.

After a few times I encountered something different. As I put the gun to this man's head I told him not to beg. Pulling the trigger, the gun went off. The man's education spread along the plastic on the floor. I could not believe it. I was in shock. It was not the first time I had killed somebody. I was not ready for the gun to be loaded this time. Covered in a fine mist of blood I heard the voice of Aurelius in my head.

"Good job. Now leave the apartment. Your work for today is done."

Still in shock I gathered myself and left. What the fuck did I get myself into. I walked to a gas station to get cigarettes. I needed one after that. Walking into the store I asked for a pack of menthol 100's and a lighter. I was getting paid yet still slept in a motel. I did not know how much money was on the credit card. Yet it always seemed to be enough. I did not want to risk it with an apartment. That would be too egregious. Plus, I like moving around.

I had just killed a man. Being in the same place always made me paranoid. The commands from Aurelius or Dr Whittaker had ceased. For the moment. Without the voices I did not know what to do. I spent my time getting drunk and watching tv at the motels. This was what it was like being a schizophrenic. All but in name.

My voice the only in my head. It was a relief yet I was used to the before. I felt lonely. Bored even. Not that I looked forward to killing another man. I wanted a purpose. The voices gave me one. Without them I was just a drunk.

Dr. Whittaker told me my parents were long dead by the time I killed their doppelgangers. I wondered what he was doing if not commanding me? I wondered if he told me the truth? Why should I trust him? To tell you the truth I really did not. I just did not want to die.

One day a few weeks later, I heard the voice again. Aurelius, Dr. Whittaker, whichever one. They told me to go to the same apartment again. Number 105. The knock was the same. The man who answered the door this time was the same. The only difference was who was tied to the chair. Still blindfolded. Still begging for their life as soon as I walked in. No gun on the table this tine. This time it was a knife. Fuck.

The voice told me to pick up the knife. So I did. They then told me to stab the man. Still begging for his life I grabbed his hair. Pulled his head back and attempted to plunge the knife into the man's heart. He screamed with all his life as the blade pushed back into the handle. A trick knife. Of fucking course.

The voices told me I was done with the task and to leave. So I did. This meeting left me with anxiety. Would the knife be switched out one day? Most likely. I hated to think of the day I feel a man's life ebb out again. Murdering the imposter parents was a play by Dr. Whittaker. Just as these whole meetings. I had to prepare myself. The truth was however, I would never be ready.

For weeks I poked a man with a fake knife. On the third week however the knife did not go blade into handle.

"Oh shit!"

I said as I was covered in blood. The man's screams echoing throughout the room. Resounding fear pulsated blood across the blade as I withdrew the knife and stabbed him again. Again and again. He grunted and coughed up blood as he died. The plastic covered in a pool of blood. I was covered in blood. It was everywhere. The voices told me I did a good job and to leave. First I was to shower.

There was a change of clothes in the bathroom for me. I washed the blood of this random man off me. Got dressed and left. What the fuck was I doing? Killing people for money on a credit card just so I could live? For what? What was the purpose? Why did they have to go through the mental torture of an unloaded gun? Or a prank knife? This made no sense to me. Yet these voices became my higher power. We were not to question our higher powers.

Dr. Whittaker, Aurelius, my Gods. They had the control of whether these men died. Not me. Yet I was a pawn in this game. Just as last time, the voices stopped for a while. I changed motels and got drunk again. This new handheld game system had come out. So I used the credit card to get one. I needed a hobby instead of mentally torturing random ass men for weeks. Before I finally killed them. Having this outlet was nice. I bought two games for it. A platformer and a virtual trading card game. It kept my time busy until the next time Dr. Whittaker would call for me to kill again. What an experiment.

What the fuck did I know? Barely anything. Twiddling my thumbs on the directional buttons I waited for the card game to load. I had switched motels again. I did not know if the police were in on this with the Dr. I did not want to find out. As the days passed without Dr. Whittaker calling to me, I began to grow paranoid.

Would I be in the chair next? What was the point of these killings? Did they owe money? Who knew? obviously not me. I had tortured multiple men for weeks at a time. Then I finally killed them. Playing my game took my mind off of the murders for a time. That is until I heard the voice in my head.

“Proceed to apartment 105 again. Your task will be waiting for you.”

“Fuck!”

I thought. Another torture.

Setting down my game I left the motel and walked to my destination. The walk to the complex was filled with thoughts about what I would see. For certain it would be a new man, begging for his life.

I arrived at the apartments. Walked to 105 and repeated the knock. The door opened to the same silent man, motioning for me to come inside. Dr Whittaker instructed me to go into the other bedroom this time. Something different. I opened the door and saw a woman laying on a bed in the middle of the room.

"You are to copulate with her to completion."

Dr. Whittaker informed me.

I was at a loss for words. For one, this body laid completely silent and blindfolded but not restrained. I asked out loud if she was okay. No response. She was alive. I could tell by her breathing. Her chest rising calmly. Up and down. I could not do this. I tried to talk to the lady. She stayed silent.

"What if I don't?"

I asked Dr. Whittaker.

"Then you will be next in the chair."

He responded.

"Shit."

I pulled down my pants and boxers. Stood over the woman and proceeded to jerk off to get an erection. I could not do it. After 5 minutes I decided I would have to go in soft. Laying on top of the woman I inserted my half flaccid penis into her. She began to silently sob behind the blindfold. I tried my best to cum as fast as possible.

"Ugghh!"

I ejaculated into her and sank into her. I whispered

"I'm sorry."

To her. She cried.

"You may now leave."

The voice in my head instructed me. So I put my clothes back on and left. What was the point of this? Just to see how obedient they could make a slave? That was all I was, a slave. Walking down the street away from the apartments, all I could think about was that girl sobbing. I did not know her from a can of paint. Yet nobody deserved that. I was becoming a monster. A dog that followed the will of its masters. What a life.

Making it back to the motel I booted up my game and played. I needed to get my mind off the fact I just raped somebody. Technically I was raped too. We both were. I did not consent. I was forced. My game was barely taking my mind off of it. So I got up and went for a walk around the city.

Beautiful Cicada East. Who knew that they walked among a monster in me. I was dangerous. A weapon formed to serve its purpose. Listening to the voices in my head. I hated it. He, a man needed to survive and this way was forced upon me. Very slowly I became a machine. Losing my humanity one person at a time. I had blood on my hands and dick. A terrible reality. I hated it. I hopped into a gas station to grab some beer. I also needed a cigarette. Paying with the card I walked out with a suitcase and a full pack of menthol 100's.

With that, I ended my walk and went back to the motel. Cracking open one I let the liquid go over my tongue. The bitter flavor welcoming. It was the color of amber. I needed to wash my memories away for the night. Booting my game I drank another and another. This went on for the whole night. Playing my game and getting drunk. These trials were hard. What was my purpose? Wherever Dr. Whittaker worked sponsored serial killers.

I was confused. Bringing my attention back to the level I was on I jumped over an enemy. This game reminiscent of one from my childhood. The beer kept flowing one after another. Out of all my crimes having to rape that woman was the worst. She was crying while I was inside her. What was the point of all this? Bubbled in my head. I did not know what I was doing. I was just following orders.

Dr. Whittaker told me I would end up in the chair if I did not do what he told me to. This chip in my brain feeding him into my head. I wish it would go away. I was not schizophrenic. I was brainwashed. My whole identity based around this chip. Dr. Whittaker said this was implanted through my soft spot. So did that mean everything I ever did was through thought control?

My inner voice combated with one from another person. It was crazy to think I rarely made a choice in my life. Another beer. Time to smoke a cigarette. I got up and set my handheld down. I had died. Walking toward the door of the motel I heard a knock. My heart froze. I did not know who was at the door. I walked to the door guarded. With a sigh I looked through the peephole. Nothing.

My faded self went back to grab the smokes. I heard another knock. This time I jumped up. I had no weapon except for my fists. I quietly slinked towards the door. As I stepped over beer cans I started to turn the knob. As the door opened I jumped out. Fists ready.

"You fucking with me!?"

Nothing. Nobody. Zilch. I looked everywhere. It was not until I looked down that's when I saw it. A piece of paper. A business card, laying on the ground in front of my feet. I leaned down to pick it up. On it a new address, seemingly to a house this time. Not much different would be in store I thought. I was wrong. I made my way to the house. It was in a worn down neighborhood on the north side. Both houses next to it were vacant. The front windows boarded on one of them. The others were broken. Walking up to the door I repeated the knock. A woman answered the door this time. I went in as she stayed silent. Dr. Whittaker's voice rang in my head.

"First door on the right."

I walked down a hallway and found the door. Walking in I saw a glass of water on a table in the middle of the room. It was overshadowed by another man tied to a chair. He sat blindfolded. Dr. Whittaker phoned in again.

"Make him drink the water."

Oh shit. This was going to be rough.

"Who's here?"

The man let out.

"Hey buddy. It's just me I'm not going to hurt you."

"I don't know who the fuck you are. What do you want from me?"

"I just need you to take a drink from this glass."

"I ain't drinking outta shit!"

I had to come up with a way to get this man to drink. Looking around the room I found a funnel. If he would not drink, I would force him to. Striking the man on the head until he stopped resisting, I forced the funnel into his mouth. Grabbing the glass cup of water, I poured it down his throat.

He coughed and sputtered. Semi conscious. I heard a voice in my head tell me to leave then. So I did. I was becoming a slave. A slave to this Dr. Whittaker and whoever he worked for. My body was no longer mine. Through these tests I have proven that. Was there anything I could do to get autonomy back? I needed to go back to the motel and have a beer. I was drinking so much I began to shit blood. I shrugged it off. I was here for a purpose not a complaint. I could say I hated it here. Close enough to the truth. I was a pawn in a game of chess. Who I was playing against… I had no idea.

Back at the motel I drank until I passed out. A regular occurrence. Why I had to force feed that man water I again had no idea. I did what I was told. They had gotten me out of the hospital. I owed them that at least. I needed to go back to sleep. So I did. I woke up the next day to the day off. I had no voices in my head give me any instructions in the morning. I decided I would spend the day walking around the city. Ol' Cicada East. Boring for the most part. Except for my new job.

Who were these people Dr. Whittaker kept having me meet? What did they do to deserve such treatment? This was all one big experiment. I had no idea what they hoped to learn from me. Or how long I could keep this up. The past few weeks being a fever dream. What even was my title? Mob enforcer? I needed sex. I had not had dick since all this started. I wanted consensual sex. I craved it. That being said, was a prostitute consensual? Well they had a job and so did I. I made it up in my mind to call one. Going onto a back pages website I found a plethora of choices. After sorting through I settled on one. An ebony man with a cute smile. I sent him a message. To my surprise he replied within the hour.

"Hey sexy."

He replied.

He had not even seen a picture of me. How disingenuous. I hate it here. Anyway I invited him over to the motel. He charged 100 an hour. Easy to put on the card they gave me. I just had to go to an atm. There was a gas station a five minute walk away from where I was staying. I went and withdrew 200 dollars. I only planned on spending one hour with him. I just liked to carry around cash. I did not want Dr. Whittaker to know what I was buying all the time. Like I could hide it. They had a chip in my brain. Either way I got the cash.

He said he would be over within the hour. Soon enough there was a knock at the door proceeded by a message. He was here. I opened the door to be greeted by two men.

"What the fuck? I thought I only ordered one?"

Before I knew it, I was on my ass. I had been decked in the face.

"If you want to live give us the money."

One had said.

"It's In my wallet."

They proceeded to flip me over and take my wallet.

"No please, leave the wallet."

"Fuck you!"

They said as they kicked me.

"Thanks for the wallet. If you call the cops we know where you stay."

Not that it mattered. After this I would be at a new motel. They left with the wallet. Credit card and all.

"Fuck… fuck me. God damn it."

How was I supposed to get anything now? On the bright side Dr. Whittaker would have seen everything through the chip. Hopefully. I still did not know how it all worked. I got no message as I lay on the floor. The door still lightly a jar. I got up to close it. I could not believe I was just robbed. What was I to do without any access to money? I needed Dr. Whittaker to contact me asap. Without anything left to do I decided I would just lock the door and sleep this off. I had rented this motel for around a week. I still had time left to figure something out. With that, I passed out. My face bruised.

That night I tossed and turned. The day weighing heavily in my dreams. I was stressed when I should have had a momentary respite. I awoke covered in sweat. The covers overheating me.

"Ugghh."

I wondered what time it was. I checked the alarm clock next to me. 6:15 it said. I had slept all night. It was not until two days later that Dr. Whittaker contacted me. Those two days I barely had tap water. I was starving. I opened the door to the room and found a card on the ground. Another call to work. This time it was to an abandoned warehouse. I got ready to leave when I heard a voice in my head. It was Dr. Whittaker.

"I have a special assignment for you today. Go to the address on the card. Your job is there."

He said nothing about the robbery. Great, just great. Hopefully the contact at the warehouse had another card for me. I walked to the address given to me. It took about 45 minutes. In that time, I thought about what this next assignment would be. Luckily, I had a pack of cigarettes and my phone. The robbers did not take them. After finishing my second cigarette I made it to the destination.

The warehouse looked decrepit and rundown. The parking lot was empty. I had to go to the back to find an entrance. It was a single door. Unlocked. Once inside I went up a flight of stairs. There I saw my contact. She did not speak. The voice in my head piped up.

"After this trial you will have your card back."

"What?! How?"

I was left with no explanation. I had to enter the room across from me. The contact escorted me. Once in the other room my jaw dropped. Strapped to two tables were the men who robbed me. On a table next to them sat wood working equipment. The voice spoke to me again.

"Do what you wish to them. Just make sure they do not leave here alive."

With that I walked over to the men. They both had gags in their mouths. Squirming and moaning, once they saw me their eyes filled with a perplexed mixture of fear and disbelief.

"MMmmHHHHhh!"

They both struggled against the bonds.

"Hey boys?"

I greeted them. They both grew more agitated. The man on the right of me had tears in his eyes. The other indignation pierced from his gaze. I walked over to the table of equipment. On it was a drill, a saw, gator cables and a hammer. I guess it was odd for all these things to be together here. Yet I saw an opportunity and took it. I picked up the electric drill and walked over to the man that had punched me.

"You're last."

I said. I then proceeded to the second man. His accomplice. I placed the drill bit on his shin and pulled the trigger. His screams were heard through the gag. Once done, I went after the other shin. He still screamed. The gag muffling his cries.

"Oh yea? How does it feel to get fucked?"

"MMMHGGG!"

Was the response. I then went back to the table of equipment and grabbed the hammer. I beat his shins to fragments all the while he screamed. Then I grabbed the saw and cut into the broken bones. With each pull the man cried out more and more. I did not even know his name. all he was to me was another test by Dr. Whittaker.

The man's legs come off with a wet sound. He was comatose at this point. Nonresponsive.

"Well, what do you think?"

I asked the first man. He just wept. Fear in his cries. Surprisingly this torture brought joy to my heart. Fuck these guys. The trials having changed my personality. I had become more sadistic. Less caring. I watched as the man cried. Sobbing. Probably for his mother. Fuck him. I placed the saw down and ruminated on what else I could grab. This time it was the hammer again. Walking over to the man remaining, he began to scream.

"Hush Hush now."

I told him. As his eyes filled with terror brought the hammer down between them. With one deft strike the man was dead. His partner losing blood from his stumps. He would be dead soon. The voice in my head began to speak.

"Good Job! Now go back to the contact for your wallet they took from you."

"Hell yea!" I thought. As I walked to the first floor where the contact was, she was waiting for me. A silent pass took place. She handed me my wallet and I asked no questions. Happy to have my pay card back. I felt like an executioner. Maybe that was my new title. Executioner of fucked up medical experiments. Either way, I was back to base. Finally, I was allowed to return to the motel.

I wondered what happened to the bodies after I was done? I would not dare look into it too much. This whole shit screamed sketchy beyond my understanding. I made my walk back to where I stayed. My mind excited about the last trip I went on. What was I to question. I got revenge. Obviously these people had me in their last thoughts. No way it was random that they got the same people that robbed me. What a coincidence. Either way the mission was completed.

I would say thank God, but who was God amongst people like this? At least I had the card back. I needed a beer. With all this going on I had become an alcoholic. Maybe I was to die to cirrhosis. If so, at least I made my self useful.

Actually, no fuck that. Just because I am working for Whittaker does not mean I have to live like shit. I am going to use this money to get a permanent place. I mean it did not seem the card had a limit to it anyway. Might as well enjoy my time with this chip in my head.

"Good choice."

Was what I heard inside my head.

"What the fuck?"

They want me to be happy?

"Yes indeed."

The voice responded

"Life is what you make it."

"Why make me go through these trials then?"

"I was reliving your trauma. It was a manifestation of your position in life. How you viewed yourself."

I was confused, happy and angry all at the same time. Mainly relieved. I could live a normal life. Did I want that though? Deep down maybe I craved violence. No!

"How do I go about doing anything beneficial to my life?"

I craved assurance that nothing bad would happen to me for my actions.

"You know that's not going to happen."

The voice was right. I needed to learn from my actions.

"You, still face more trials as life goes on. That was the deal your parents signed."

"Deal?"

That was the last I heard of Dr. Whittaker. A new voice had appeared in my thoughts. My own. I walked back to my current motel. Stopping by a gas station to buy a celebratory beer, my card declined.

www.ingramcontent.com/pod-product-compliance
Lightning Source LLC
Chambersburg PA
CBHW030647110726
47901CB00002B/605

* 9 7 9 8 9 9 3 4 4 6 7 0 7 *